RAINBOW magic ®
THE TREASURY

Special thanks to
Narinder Dhami and
Sue Bentley

ORCHARD BOOKS
96 Leonard Street, London EC2A 4XD
Hachette Children's Books
Level 17/207 Kent St, Sydney NSW 2000
First published in Great Britain in this abridged edition in 2005
Text © Working Partners Limited 2003 and 2005
Rainbow Magic is a registered trademark of Working Partners Limited.
Series created by Working Partners Limited, London W6 0QT
Cover and black and white line illustrations © Georgie Ripper 2003 and 2005
The right of Georgie Ripper to be identified as the illustrator
of this work has been asserted by her in accordance
with the Copyright, Designs and Patents Act, 1988.
A CIP catalogue record for this book is available
from the British Library.
ISBN 1 84616 047 2
1 3 5 7 9 10 8 6 4 2
Printed in China

RAINBOW magic ®

THE TREASURY

by Daisy Meadows

Cover and black line illustrations
by Georgie Ripper

ORCHARD BOOKS

The
Fairyland
Palace

Maze

Forest

Orchard

Black
Pot

Meadow

Tower

Beach

Rockpools

Rainspell Island

Jack Frost's Ice Castle

Tom Goodfellow's House

Mrs Merry's Cottage

Willow Tree

Stream

Field

Mermaid Cottage

Town

Harbour

Dolphin Cottage

Cold winds blow and thick ice form,
I conjure up this fairy storm.
To seven corners of the mortal world
the Rainbow Fairies will be hurled!

I curse every part of Fairyland,
with a frosty wave of my icy hand.
For now and always, from this fateful day,
Fairyland will be cold and grey!

Contents

Ruby
the Red
Fairy

Chapter One

Ruby the Red Fairy

"Look, Dad!" said Rachel Walker. She pointed across the blue-green sea at the rocky island ahead of them.

"Is that Rainspell Island?" she asked.

Her dad nodded. "Yes. Our holiday is about to begin!"

The waves slapped against the side of the ferry and Rachel felt her heart thump with excitement.

Suddenly, a few fat raindrops plopped down onto her head. "Oh!" she gasped.

Rachel's mum grabbed her hand.

"Let's go inside," she said.

"Isn't that strange?" Rachel said.

"The sun is still shining!"

"Let's hope the rain stops before we arrive," said Mr Walker.

Rachel looked out of the window. A girl was standing alone on the deck, staring up at the sky. Rachel slipped back outside to see what was so interesting.

High above them was the most amazing rainbow that Rachel had ever seen. One end of the rainbow was far out to sea. The other seemed to fall somewhere on Rainspell Island.

"Isn't it perfect?" the dark-haired girl whispered to Rachel.

"Yes, it is," Rachel agreed. "Are you going to Rainspell on holiday?"

The girl nodded. "I'm Kirsty Tate," she said.

Rachel smiled. "I'm Rachel Walker. We're staying at Mermaid Cottage," she added.

"And we're at Dolphin Cottage," said Kirsty. "Do you think we might be near each other?"

"I hope so," Rachel replied. She had a feeling she was going to like Kirsty.

The ferry sailed into Rainspell's tiny harbour. Seagulls flew around them, and fishing boats bobbed on the water.

"There you are, Rachel!" called Mrs Walker.

Rachel saw her mum and dad coming on to the deck. "Mum, Dad, this is Kirsty," she said. "She's staying at Dolphin Cottage."

"That's right next door to ours," said Mr Walker. "I remember seeing it on the map."

Rachel and Kirsty looked at each other in delight.

"I'd better go and find my mum and dad," said Kirsty. She looked round. "Oh, here they are."

Kirsty's mum and dad came over to say hello. Then the ferry docked, and everyone began to leave the boat.

Mermaid Cottage and Dolphin Cottage were right next to the beach. Rachel loved her bedroom in the attic. From the window,

she could see the waves rolling onto the sand. A shout from outside made her look down. Kirsty was standing under the window, waving at her.

"Let's go and explore the beach!" she called. Rachel dashed outside. Seaweed lay in piles on the sand, and there were tiny pink and white shells dotted about.

"I love it here already!" Rachel shouted happily above the noise of the seagulls.

12

"Me too," Kirsty said. She pointed up at the sky. "Look, the rainbow's still there."

Sure enough, the rainbow glowed brightly among the fluffy white clouds.

"Have you heard the story about the pot of gold at the end of the rainbow?" Kirsty asked.

Rachel nodded. "Yes, but that's just in fairy stories," she said.

Kirsty grinned. "Maybe. Let's go and find out for ourselves!"

"OK," Rachel agreed.

They rushed back to tell their parents they were going for a walk. Then they set off along the lane. It led away from the beach, towards a small wood.

Rachel kept looking up at the rainbow. She was worried that it would start to fade now that the rain had stopped. But the colours stayed clear and bright. "It looks like the end of the rainbow is over there," Kirsty said. "Come on!" And she hurried towards the trees.

The wood was cool and green after the heat of the sun. Rachel and Kirsty followed a winding path until they came to a clearing. Then they both stopped and stared.

The rainbow shone down onto the grass through a gap in the trees. And there, at the rainbow's end, lay an old, black pot.

✿ ✿ ✿

"There really is a pot of gold!" Kirsty exclaimed.

"It could just be a cooking pot," Rachel said. "Some campers might have left it behind."

But Kirsty shook her head. "I don't think so," she said. "It looks really old."

The pot was sitting on the grass, upside down.

"Let's have a closer look," said Kirsty. She tried to turn it over. "It's heavy!" she gasped. Rachel went to help her. They pushed and pushed at the pot. This time it moved, just a little.

"Let's try again," Kirsty panted.

"Are you ready, Rachel?"

Tap! Tap! Tap!

"What was that?" Rachel gasped.

"I don't know," whispered Kirsty.

Tap! Tap!

Kirsty looked down. "I think it's coming from inside the pot!"

Rachel's eyes opened wide. "Are you sure?" She bent down, and put her ear to the pot. Tap! Tap! Then, to her amazement, Rachel heard a tiny voice.

"Help!" it called. "Help me!"

Rachel grabbed Kirsty's arm. "Did you hear that?"

Kirsty nodded. "Quick!" she said. "We must turn the pot over!"

Rachel and Kirsty pushed at the pot as hard as they could. It began to rock from side to side.

"We're nearly there!" Rachel panted.

Suddenly, the pot rolled on to its side. A shower of sparkling red dust flew out of it. And there, right in the middle of the glittering cloud, was a tiny girl with wings!

Rachel and Kirsty watched in wonder as the tiny girl fluttered in the sunlight, her delicate wings sparkling

with all the colours of the rainbow.

"Oh, Rachel!" Kirsty whispered. "It's a fairy…"

❀ ❀ ❀

15

The fairy fluttered just above Rachel and Kirsty. Her short, silky dress was the colour of strawberries. Red earrings glowed in her ears. Her golden hair was plaited with tiny red roses, and she wore crimson slippers on her little feet.

She waved her wand and a shower of sparkling red fairy dust floated softly down to the ground. Where it landed, all sorts of red flowers appeared with a pop!

Rachel and Kirsty watched open-mouthed. It really and truly was a fairy.

"This is like a dream," Rachel said.

"I always believed in fairies," said Kirsty. "But I never thought I'd see one!"

The fairy flew towards them. "Oh, thank you so much!" she called in a tiny, silvery voice. "I'm free at last!" She glided down, and landed on Kirsty's hand.

Kirsty gasped. The fairy felt lighter and softer than a butterfly.

"I was beginning to think I'd never get out of that pot!" said the fairy. "Tell me your names, quickly. There's so much to be done, and we must get started right away."

Rachel wondered what the fairy meant. "I'm Rachel," she said.

"And I'm Kirsty," said Kirsty.

"I'm the Red Rainbow Fairy – but you can call me Ruby," the fairy replied.

"Ruby..." Kirsty breathed. "A Rainbow Fairy..."

"Yes," said Ruby. "I have six sisters: Amber, Saffron, Fern, Sky, Izzy and Heather. One for each colour of the rainbow, you see. It's our job to put all the different colours into Fairyland," she explained.

"Why were you shut up inside that old pot?" said Rachel.

"And where are your sisters?" Kirsty added.

Ruby's wings drooped and her eyes filled with tears. "I don't know," she said. "Something terrible has happened in Fairyland. We need your help!"

"Of course we'll help you!" Kirsty said.

Ruby wiped her eyes. "Thank you!" she said. "First I must show you something. Follow me – as quickly as you can!" She flew into the air, her wings shimmering in the sunshine. Rachel and Kirsty followed Ruby across the clearing.

The fairy stopped by a pond under a willow tree. "Look!" she said. "I can show you what happened yesterday."

She flew over the pond and scattered another shower of sparkling fairy dust with her wand. The water lit up with a strange, silver light.

Rachel and Kirsty watched in astonishment as a picture appeared. It was like looking through a window into another land!

A river of brightest blue ran past hills of greenest green. Scattered on the hillsides were red and white toadstool houses. And on top of the highest hill stood a silver palace with four pink towers.

The towers were so high, their points were almost hidden by the fluffy white clouds.

Hundreds of fairies were making their way towards the palace. Rachel and Kirsty could see elves, pixies and sprites too. Everyone seemed very excited.

"Yesterday was the day of the Fairyland Midsummer Ball," Ruby explained. She pointed with her wand. "There I am, with my Rainbow sisters."

Kirsty and Rachel saw seven fairies, each dressed prettily in their own rainbow colour.

"The Midsummer Ball is very special," Ruby went on. "My sisters and I are in charge of sending out invitations."

To the sound of tinkling music, the front doors of the palace slowly opened.

"Here come King Oberon and Queen Titania," said Ruby. "The Fairy King and Queen."

Kirsty and Rachel watched as the King and Queen stepped out. The King wore a splendid golden coat and golden crown. His queen wore a silver dress and a tiara that sparkled with diamonds. Everyone cheered. After a while, the King signalled for quiet. "Fairies, elves, pixies and sprites," he began. "Welcome to the Midsummer Ball!"

The fairies clapped and cheered again.

Suddenly, a grey mist filled the picture. Kirsty and Rachel watched in alarm as all the fairies started to shiver. A loud, chilly voice shouted out, "Stop the music!"

A tall, bony figure was pushing his way through the crowd. He was dressed all in white, and there was frost on his white hair and beard. Icicles hung from his clothes. But his face was red and angry. Everyone looked scared.

"Who's that?" Rachel asked with a shiver.

"Jack Frost," said Ruby.

Jack Frost glared at the seven Rainbow Fairies. "Why wasn't I invited to the Midsummer Ball?" he asked coldly.

The Rainbow Fairies gasped in horror...

Ruby looked up from the pond picture. "Yes, we forgot to invite Jack Frost," she said.

In the pond picture, the Fairy Queen stepped forward. "You are very welcome, Jack Frost," she said. "Please stay and enjoy the ball."

But Jack Frost just looked angrier. "Too late!" he hissed. "You forgot to invite me!" He pointed a thin, icy finger at the Rainbow Fairies. "You will not forget this!" he snarled. "My spell will banish the Rainbow Fairies to the seven corners of the mortal world. From this day on, Fairyland will be without colour – for ever!"

❀ ❀ ❀

An icy wind began to blow. It picked up the seven Rainbow Fairies and spun them up into the sky. The other fairies watched in dismay.

Jack Frost turned to the King and Queen. "Your Rainbow Fairies will never return!" he cackled. He walked away, leaving a trail of icy footprints.

The Fairy Queen lifted her silver wand. "I cannot undo Jack Frost's magic completely," she cried. "But I can guide the Rainbow Fairies to a safe place where they will be rescued!"

She pointed her wand at the sky. A black pot came spinning through the stormy clouds. One by one, the Rainbow Fairies tumbled into the pot.

"Pot-at-the-end-of-the-rainbow, keep our Rainbow Fairies safely together," the Queen called. "And take them to Rainspell Island!"

The pot flew out of sight, behind a dark cloud. At once the bright colours of Fairyland began to fade, until it looked like an old black and white photograph.

"Oh no!" Kirsty gasped. The picture in the pond vanished.

"The Fairy Queen cast her own spell!" Rachel said. "She put you and your sisters in the pot, and sent you to Rainspell."

Ruby nodded. "Rainspell is a place full of magic. She knew we'd be safe here."

"But where are your sisters?" asked Kirsty. "They were in the pot too."

Ruby looked upset. "Jack Frost's spell was very strong," she said.

"As the pot spun through the sky, the wind blew my sisters out again. I was at the bottom, so I was safe. But I was trapped when the pot landed upside down."

"So your sisters are somewhere on Rainspell?" Kirsty said.

Ruby nodded. "They're scattered all over the island. Jack Frost's spell has trapped them too." She flew on to Kirsty's shoulder. "That's where you and Rachel come in."

"How?" Rachel asked.

"You found me, didn't you?" the fairy said. "So you could rescue my Rainbow sisters too! Then we can all bring colour back to Fairyland."

"Of course we'll search for your sisters," Kirsty said. "Won't we, Rachel?"

Rachel nodded.

"Oh, thank you," Ruby said happily.

"But we're only here for a week," Rachel said.

"We must get started right away," said Ruby. "First, I must take you to Fairyland to meet the King and Queen."

"You're taking us to Fairyland?" Kirsty gasped.

"But how will we get there?" Rachel said.

"We'll fly there," Ruby replied.

"But we can't fly!" Rachel pointed out.

Ruby smiled. She whirled up into the air and swirled her wand above them. Magic red fairy dust fluttered down.

Rachel and Kirsty began to feel a bit strange. Were the trees getting bigger or were they getting smaller?

They were getting smaller!

Smaller and smaller and smaller, until they were the same size as Ruby.

"I'm tiny!" Rachel laughed. She was so small, the flowers around her seemed like trees.

Kirsty twisted round to look at her back. She had shiny, delicate wings!

Ruby beamed. "Let's go!"

Rachel twitched her shoulders. Her wings fluttered, and she felt herself rise up into the air. She was quite wobbly at first!

"Help!" Kirsty yelled, as she shot up into the air. "I'm not very good at this!"

"Come on," said Ruby, taking their hands. "I'll help you." She led them up, out of the glade.

Rachel looked down on Rainspell Island. She could see the cottages next to the beach, and the harbour.

"Where is Fairyland, Ruby?" Kirsty asked.

"It's so far away, that no mortal could ever find it," Ruby said.

They flew through the clouds for a long, long time. At last Ruby turned to them and smiled. "We're here," she said.

As they flew down, Kirsty and Rachel saw places they recognised from the pond picture: the palace, the hillsides, the toadstool houses. But there were no bright colours now. Because of Jack Frost's spell, everything was a drab shade of grey. Even the air felt cold and damp.

A few fairies walked miserably across the hillsides. Their wings hung limply down their backs.

Suddenly one of the fairies looked up. "Look!" she shouted. "It's Ruby!"

At once, the fairies flew up to meet Ruby, Kirsty and Rachel.

"Have you come from Rainspell, Ruby?"

"Where are the other Rainbow Fairies?"

23

"Who are your friends?" said another fairy.

"First, we must see the King and Queen," said Ruby. "Then I will tell you everything!"

King Oberon and Queen Titania were seated on their thrones. Their palace was as grey as everywhere else in Fairyland. But they smiled warmly when Ruby arrived with Rachel and Kirsty.

"Welcome back, Ruby," said the Queen. "We have missed you."

"Your Majesties, these are my friends, Kirsty and Rachel. They believe in magic!" Ruby announced. She told everyone how Rachel and Kirsty had rescued her.

"Will you help us to find Ruby's Rainbow sisters?" the Queen asked.

"Yes, we will," Kirsty said.

"How will we know where to look?" said Rachel, feeling worried.

"Don't worry," said the Queen. "The magic you need to find each Rainbow Fairy will find you. Just wait and see."

King Oberon rubbed his beard. "You have six days of your holiday left, and six fairies to find," he said. "That's a lot of fairy-finding. You will need some special help." He nodded at one of his footmen, a plump frog in a buttoned-up jacket.

The frog hopped over to
Rachel and Kirsty and
handed them each a
tiny, silver bag.

"The bags contain
magic tools," the Queen
told them. "Open them
only when you really
need to, and you will find something to help you."

"Look!" shouted another frog footman. "Ruby is beginning to fade!"

Rachel and Kirsty looked at Ruby
in horror. The fairy was growing
paler! Her lovely dress was no
longer red but pink, and her
golden hair was turning white.
"Jack Frost's magic is still at work,"
said the King. "We cannot undo
his spell until all the Rainbow
Fairies are together again."

"Quick, Ruby!" urged the Queen. "You must return to Rainspell at
once."

Ruby, Kirsty and Rachel flew into the air.

"Don't worry!" Kirsty called. "We'll be back with all the Rainbow
Fairies very soon!"

"Good luck!" called the King and Queen.

As they flew further away from Fairyland, Ruby's colour began to
return. Soon she was bright and sparkling again.

When they reached Rainspell again, they landed in the clearing next to the old, black pot. Ruby scattered fairy dust over Rachel and Kirsty. There was a puff of glittering red smoke, and the two girls shot up to their normal size. Rachel wriggled her shoulders. Her wings had gone. "I loved being a fairy," Kirsty said. They watched as Ruby sprinkled her magic dust over the old, black pot. "What are you doing?" Rachel asked. "Jack Frost's magic means that I can't help you look for my sisters," Ruby explained. "I will wait for you here, in the pot-at-the-end-of-the-rainbow."

Suddenly the pot began to move. It rolled across the grass, and stopped under the weeping willow tree.

"The pot will be hidden under the tree," said Ruby. "I'll be safe there."

"We'd better start looking for the other Rainbow Fairies," Rachel said to Kirsty. "Where shall we start?"

Ruby shook her head. "Remember what the Queen said," she told them. "The magic will come to you." She flew into the air. "Goodbye, and good luck!"

"We'll be back soon, Ruby," said Kirsty.

"And we're going to find *all* your Rainbow sisters," Rachel promised.

Amber
the Orange Fairy

Chapter Two

Amber the Orange Fairy

"What a lovely day!" Rachel Walker cried. She and her friend, Kirsty Tate, were running along Rainspell Island's yellow, sandy beach. Their parents walked a little way behind them.

"It's a *magical* day," Kirsty added with a grin.

As they ran, they passed rock pools that shone like jewels in the sunshine.

Rachel spotted a little *splash!* in one of the pools. "There's something in there, Kirsty!" She pointed. "Let's go and look."

Kirsty's heart thumped as she gazed into the crystal clear water.

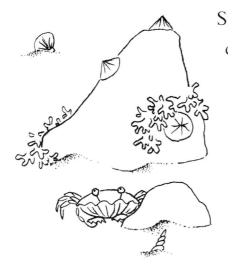

Suddenly, the water rippled. A little brown crab scuttled across the sandy bottom and vanished under a rock. Kirsty felt disappointed. "I thought it might be another Rainbow Fairy," she said.

Rachel sighed. "Never mind. We'll have to keep looking."

"Of course we will," Kirsty agreed.

Rachel looked at the shimmering blue sea. "Shall we have a swim?"

But Kirsty wasn't listening. "Look over there, by those rocks," she said.

Rachel saw something sparkling in the sunshine. She hurried over and picked up a piece of shiny purple foil.

"It's just the wrapper from a chocolate bar," she said sadly.

"Do you remember what the Fairy Queen said?" Kirsty asked.

Rachel nodded. "Let the magic come to you," she said. "You're right, Kirsty. We should wait for the magic to happen. After all, that's how we found Ruby, isn't it?" She put her beach bag on the sand. "Come on – race you into the sea!"

They rushed into the water and splashed about until they got goosebumps. Then they walked along the beach looking for shells. They found long, thin, blue shells and tiny, round, white shells. Soon their hands were full.

They had walked right round the curve of the bay. Rachel looked over her shoulder. "Look how far we've come," she said.

Kirsty stopped. A gust of wind tugged at her T-shirt and she shivered. "It's getting cold now," she said. "Shall we go back?"

"Yes, it must be nearly teatime," said Rachel.

They began to walk back along the beach. "That's funny," said Kirsty. "It's not windy here."

They looked back and saw little swirls of sand being blown around where they'd just been. The two friends looked at each other with excitement. "It's magic," Kirsty whispered. "It has to be!"

They walked back and the breeze swirled around their legs again. Then the sand began to drift to one side, as if invisible hands were pushing it away. A large scallop shell appeared, much bigger than the other shells on the beach. It was pearly white with soft orange streaks, and it was tightly closed.

The girls knelt down on the sand, spilling the little shells out of their hands. Kirsty was about to pick up the scallop shell when Rachel put out her hand. "Listen," she whispered.

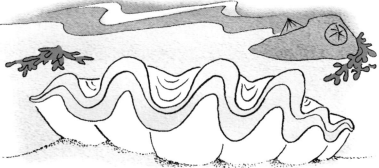

Inside the shell, a tiny, silvery voice was humming...

Very carefully, Rachel picked up the shell.

The humming stopped at once. "I mustn't be scared," said the tiny voice. "I just have to be brave, and help will come very soon."

Humm m m...

"Hello," Kirsty whispered. "Is there a fairy in there?"

"Yes!" cried the voice. "I'm Amber the Orange Fairy! Can you get me out of here?"

"Of course we will," Kirsty promised. "My name is Kirsty, and my friend Rachel is here too." She looked up at Rachel. "We've found another Rainbow Fairy!"

"Quick," Rachel said. "Let's get the shell open." She took hold of the scallop shell and tried to pull the two halves apart. Nothing happened.

"Try again," said Kirsty. She and Rachel each grasped one half of the shell and tugged. But the shell stayed tightly shut.

"What's happening?" Amber called.

"We can't open the shell," Kirsty said.

"But we'll think of something." She turned to Rachel. "If we find a piece of driftwood, we could use it to open the shell."

Rachel glanced around. "I can't see any driftwood," she said. "We could try tapping the shell on a rock."

"But that might hurt Amber," Kirsty said.

Suddenly Rachel remembered something. "What about the magic bags the Fairy Queen gave us?"

31

"Of course!" Kirsty put her face close to the shell again. "Amber, we're going to look in our magic bags."

"OK, but please hurry," Amber called.

Rachel opened her beach bag. The two magic bags were hidden under her towel. One of the bags was glowing with a golden light.

"Open it, quick," Kirsty whispered.

As Rachel undid the bag, a fountain of glittering sparks flew out.

She slid her hand into the bag. She could feel something light and soft inside. She pulled it out, scattering sparkles everywhere. It was a shimmering golden feather.

Rachel tried to use the feather to push the two halves of the shell apart. But the feather just curled up in her hand.

"Maybe we should ask Amber how to open the shell with the feather," said Rachel.

"Amber, we've looked in the magic bags," Kirsty said, "and we've found a feather."

"Oh, good!" Amber said happily.

"But we don't know what to do with it," Rachel added.

Amber laughed. It sounded like the tinkle of a tiny bell. "You tickle the shell, of course!"

"Let's give it a try," Kirsty said.

Rachel began to tickle the shell with the feather. At first nothing happened. Then they heard a soft, gritty chuckle. Then another and another. Slowly the two halves of the shell began to open.

"It's working," Kirsty gasped. "Keep tickling, Rachel!"

The shell was laughing hard now. The two halves opened wider…

And there, sitting inside the smooth, peach-coloured shell, was Amber the Orange Fairy.

"I'm free!" Amber cried joyfully.

She shot out of the shell and up into the air. Orange fairy dust floated down around Kirsty and Rachel. It turned into orange bubbles as it fell. One of the bubbles landed on Rachel's arm and burst with a tiny POP!

"The bubbles smell like oranges!" Rachel smiled.

Amber turned cartwheels through the sky. "Thank you!" she called.

She wore a shiny orange catsuit and long boots. Her flame-coloured hair was tied in a ponytail with a band of peach blossoms.

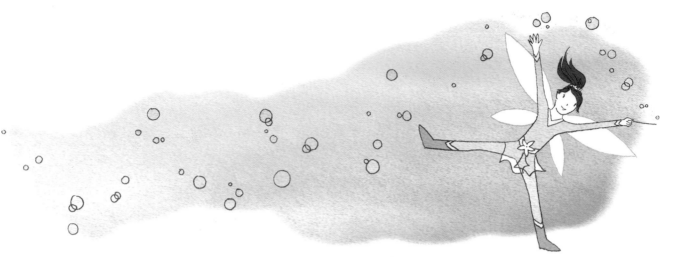

She held an orange wand tipped with gold.

"I'm so glad you found me!" Amber cried. "But who are you? And where are my Rainbow sisters?"

Suddenly she stopped. She floated down and landed softly on Rachel's hand. "I'm sorry," she said with a smile. "I've been shut up in this shell ever since Jack Frost's spell banished us from Fairyland. How did you know where to find me?"

"Kirsty and I promised your sister Ruby that we would look for all the Rainbow Fairies," Rachel told her.

"Ruby?" Amber's face lit up. "You've found Ruby?"

"Yes, she's quite safe," Rachel said. "She's in the pot-at-the-end-of-the-rainbow under a willow tree."

Amber did a backflip. "Please take me to her!" she begged.

"I'll ask our parents if we can go for a walk," Kirsty said. She ran across the beach and quickly came back. "Mum said that's fine," she panted.

"Let's go!" Amber called. She flew up and did a somersault in mid-air.

34

Rachel pulled their shorts, T-shirts and trainers out of her beach bag and both girls put them on.

"Rachel, could you bring my shell?" Amber asked.

Rachel looked surprised. "Yes, of course," she said.

"It's really comfy," Amber explained. "It will make a lovely bed for me and my sisters."

Rachel put the shell in her beach bag, and they set off with Amber sitting cross-legged on Kirsty's shoulder.

"My wings are a bit stiff after being in the shell," she said. "I don't think I can fly very far yet."

The girls reached the clearing where the pot-at-the-end-of-the-rainbow was hidden.

The pot was where they'd left it, under the weeping willow tree. But climbing out of it was a big, green frog.

"Oh no!" Rachel cried.

Where was Ruby?

Rachel dashed forward and grabbed the frog round his plump, green tummy. The frog glared at her. "What do you think you're doing?" he croaked. Rachel was so shocked, she let go of the frog.

He hopped away, looking very annoyed.

"It's a talking frog!" Kirsty gasped.

"Bertram!" Amber flew down from Kirsty's shoulder and threw her arms around the frog. "Thank goodness you're safe, Miss Amber!" said the frog.

Amber beamed at Rachel and Kirsty. "Bertram isn't an ordinary frog," she explained. "He's one of King Oberon's footmen."

"Oh, yes!" said Kirsty. "We saw the frog footmen when we went to the palace in Fairyland with Ruby."

"But they were wearing purple uniforms then," Rachel added.

"A frog in a purple uniform would not be a good idea on Rainspell Island," Bertram pointed out. "It's much better if I look like an ordinary frog."

"What are you doing here, Bertram?" asked Amber. "Where's Ruby?"

"Don't worry," Bertram replied. "Miss Ruby is safe in the pot." He looked very stern. "King Oberon sent me to Rainspell. The Cloud Fairies spotted Jack Frost's goblins sneaking out of Fairyland. We think he has sent them here to stop the Rainbow Fairies being found."

Kirsty felt a shiver run down her spine. "Jack Frost's goblins?" she said.

"They're his servants," Amber explained. Her wings trembled and she looked very scared.

"They want to keep Fairyland cold and grey!"

"I'll look after you, Miss Amber," Bertram croaked.

Suddenly a shower of red fairy dust shot out of the pot. Ruby fluttered out. "Amber!" she shouted joyfully. "They found you!"

"Ruby!" Amber called. She cartwheeled towards her sister. The air around them fizzed with tiny red flowers and orange bubbles.

"Thank you, Kirsty and Rachel," said Ruby. She and Amber floated down to them, holding hands. "It's so good to have Amber back safely."

37

"What about you?" Rachel asked. "Have you been all right in the pot?"

Ruby nodded. "I'm fine now that Bertram is here," she replied. "I've been making the pot into a fairy home."

"I've brought my shell with me," Amber said. "It will make a lovely bed for us. Show her, Rachel."

Rachel took the peach-coloured shell out of her bag.

"It's beautiful," said Ruby. She smiled at Rachel and Kirsty. "Would you like to come and see our new home?"

"But the pot's too small for Kirsty and me to get inside," Rachel pointed out. Then she began to tingle with excitement. "Are you going to make us fairy size again?"

Ruby nodded. She and Amber flew over the girls' heads, showering them with fairy dust. Rachel and Kirsty started to shrink, just as they had done before. Soon they were tiny, the same size as Ruby and Amber.

"Being a fairy is the best thing ever," Kirsty said happily. She twisted round to look at her silvery wings.

"Yes, it is," Rachel agreed. Bertram hopped over to the pot. "I'll wait outside," he croaked. Ruby took Rachel's hand, and Amber took Kirsty's. Then the fairies led them towards the pot.

Rachel and Kirsty fluttered through the air, dodging a butterfly that was as big as they were. Its wings felt like velvet as they brushed gently past it.

"I'm getting better at flying!" Kirsty laughed as she landed neatly on the edge of the pot. She looked down eagerly.

The pot was full of sunlight. There were little chairs made from twigs tied with blades of grass. Each chair had a cushion made from a berry. Rugs of bright green leaves covered the floor.

"Shall we fetch the shell?" said Rachel. When they flew out of the pot, Bertram was already pushing the shell towards them across the grass. "Here you are," he croaked. The shell seemed very heavy now that Rachel and Kirsty were the same size as Ruby and Amber. Bertram helped them to heave it into the pot.

Ruby lined it with sweet-smelling rose petals.

"I wish I could live here too!" said Kirsty.

Ruby turned to her sister. "Do you like it, Amber?" she asked.

"It's beautiful," Amber replied. "It reminds me of our house back in Fairyland. I miss it so much."

"Well, I can show you Fairyland," Ruby said, "even though we can't go back there yet. Follow me."

Bertram was still on guard next to the pot when they flew out again. "Where are you going?" he croaked.

"To the magic pond," Ruby replied. "Come with us." She sprinkled her magic dust over Rachel and Kirsty. Quickly, they grew back to their normal size.

They went over to the pond. Ruby flew above the water,

scattering fairy dust. Just like before, a picture began to appear.

"Fairyland!" Amber cried, gazing into the water. Fairyland still looked sad and chilly. The palace, the toadstool houses, the flowers and the trees were all drab and grey. Suddenly a cold breeze rippled the surface of the water, and the picture began to fade.

"What's happening?" Kirsty whispered.

Another picture was taking shape in the pond – a thin, grinning face with icicles hanging from his beard.

"It's Jack Frost!" Ruby gasped. As she spoke, the air turned icy cold and the edges of the pool began to freeze.

"What's happening?" Rachel asked, shivering.

"This is bad news," said Bertram. "It means that Jack Frost's goblins are close by!"

The whole pond froze over. Jack Frost's grinning face faded away.

"Follow me," Bertram ordered. He hopped over to a large bush. "We'll hide here."

"Maybe we should go back to the pot," said Ruby.

"Not if the goblins are close by," said Bertram. "We mustn't let them know where the pot is."

The two girls crouched down behind the bush next to Bertram. Ruby and Amber huddled together on Kirsty's shoulder. It was getting colder and colder. Rachel and Kirsty couldn't stop their teeth chattering.

"What are the goblins like?" Rachel whispered.

"They're bigger than us," said Amber, trembling.

"And they have ugly faces and hooked noses and big feet," Ruby added.

"Hush, Miss Ruby," Bertram croaked. "I can hear something."

Rachel saw a hook-nosed shadow flit across the clearing towards them. She grabbed Kirsty's arm. Suddenly the leaves rustled right next to them. They almost jumped out of their skins.

"Oi!" said a gruff voice, sounding very close.

"What do you think you're doing?"

Rachel and Kirsty held their breath.

"Nothing," said another gruff voice.

"Goblins!" Amber whispered in Kirsty's ear.

"You stood on my toe," said the first goblin.

"No, I didn't," snapped the other goblin.

"Yes, you did! Keep your big feet to yourself!"

"Well, at least my nose isn't as big as yours!"

The bush shook even more. It sounded as if the goblins were pushing and shoving each other.

"Get out of my way!" one of them shouted. "Ow!"

Rachel and Kirsty looked at each other in alarm. What if the goblins found them there?

"Come on," said one of the goblins. "Jack Frost will be cross if we don't find these fairies. You know he wants us to stop them getting back to Fairyland."

"Well, they're not here, are they?" grumbled the other. "Let's try somewhere else."

The voices died away. The leaves stopped rustling. Suddenly the air felt warm again. There was a cracking sound as the frozen pond began to melt.

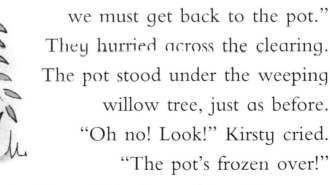

"They've gone," Bertram croaked. "Quick, we must get back to the pot." They hurried across the clearing. The pot stood under the weeping willow tree, just as before. "Oh no! Look!" Kirsty cried. "The pot's frozen over!"

The top of the pot was covered with a thick sheet of ice. No one, not even a fairy, could get inside.

43

"Oh no!" Ruby gasped. "The goblins must have passed really close by!"

She flew over to the pot with Amber right behind her. They drummed on the ice with their tiny fists. But it was too thick for them to break through.

"Shall we try, Rachel?" asked Kirsty. "We could smash the ice with a stick."

But Bertram had another idea. "Stand back, please, everyone," he said. Suddenly, he leaped forward with a mighty hop. He jumped straight at the sheet of ice, kicking out with his webbed feet. But the ice did not break. "Try again," he panted.

He jumped forward again and hit the ice. This time, there was a loud cracking sound. One more jump, 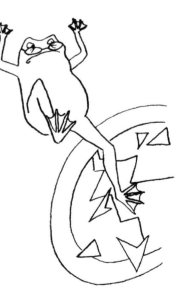 and the ice shattered into little pieces. Some of it fell inside the pot. Rachel and Kirsty rushed over to fish them out before they melted.

"There you are," Bertram croaked.

"Thank you, Bertram," Ruby called. She and Amber flew down and hugged the frog.

Bertram looked pleased. "Just doing my job, Miss Ruby," he said. "You and Miss Amber must stay very close to the pot from now on. It's dangerous for you to go too far."

"We've got to say goodbye to our friends first," Amber told him.

She flew into the air, smiling at Rachel and Kirsty. "Thank you a thousand times."

"We'll see you again soon," said Rachel.

"When we've found your next Rainbow sister," Kirsty added.

"Good luck!" said Ruby. "We'll be waiting here for you." She took her sister's hand, and they flew over to the pot. The two fairies turned to wave at the girls and disappeared inside.

"Don't worry," Bertram said. "I'll look after them."

"We know you will," Rachel said.

She and Kirsty walked out of the wood. "I'm glad Ruby isn't on her own any more," said Rachel.

"I didn't like those goblins," Kirsty said with a shudder. "I hope they don't come back again."

They made their way back to the beach. Their parents were packing away their towels.

"We were just coming to look for you," said Mr Walker.

"Are we going home now?" Rachel asked.

Mr Walker nodded. "It's turned very chilly," he said.

As he spoke, a cold breeze swirled around Rachel and Kirsty. They shivered and looked up at the sky. The sun had disappeared behind a thick, black cloud.

"Jack Frost's goblins are still here!" Kirsty gasped.

"You're right," Rachel agreed. "Let's hope Bertram can keep Ruby and Amber safe while we look for the other Rainbow Fairies!"

Saffron the Yellow Fairy

Chapter Three

Saffron the Yellow Fairy

"Over here, Kirsty!" Rachel called.

She and Kirsty were running across one of the emerald green fields on Rainspell Island. Buttercups and daisies dotted the grass.

"Don't go too far!" Kirsty's mum called.

Kirsty caught up with her friend. Rachel was standing on the bank of a rippling stream. "What have you found, Rachel? Is it another Rainbow Fairy?"

"I'm not sure," said Rachel. "I thought I heard something."

Kirsty's face lit up. "Maybe there's a fairy in the stream?"

Rachel knelt down and put her ear close to the water. Kirsty crouched down too and listened hard.

The sun glittered on the water as it splashed over big, shiny pebbles.

Then they heard a tiny bubbling voice. "Follow me..." it gurgled. "Follow me..."

48

"Did you hear that?" Rachel gasped.

"Yes," said Kirsty, her eyes wide. "It must be a magic stream!"

"Maybe the stream will lead us to the Yellow Fairy!" said Rachel.

Kirsty's parents had stopped to admire the stream too. "Which way now?" asked Mr Tate.

"Let's go this way," Kirsty said, pointing along the bank.

A kingfisher flew up from a twig. Butterflies as bright as jewels fluttered among the reeds.

"Everything on Rainspell Island is so beautiful," said Kirsty's mum. "I'm glad we still have five days of holiday left!"

Yes, Rachel thought, and five Rainbow Fairies still to find! Ruby the Red Fairy and Amber the Orange Fairy were already safe in the pot-at-the-end-of-the-rainbow.

The girls ran on ahead. As they followed the stream, the sun went behind a big, dark cloud. A chilly breeze ruffled the girls' hair.

Kirsty saw that some of the leaves on the trees were turning brown, even though it wasn't autumn. "It looks like Jack Frost's goblins are still around," she warned Rachel.

"I know." Rachel shivered. "They'll do anything to stop the Rainbow Fairies getting back to Fairyland."

The stream ran through a meadow. A herd of black and white cows were grazing at the water's edge.

"Aren't they lovely?" Kirsty said.

Suddenly the cows ran off towards the other end of the field.

Rachel and Kirsty looked at each other in surprise. What was going on?

There was a loud buzzing noise. A small angry shape came whizzing through the air, straight towards them!

Rachel almost jumped out of her skin. "It's a bee!"

"Run!" Kirsty cried.

Rachel tore through the meadow with Kirsty beside her, their feet pounding the grass.

"Keep running, girls," called Mr Tate, catching up with them. "That bee seems to be following us!"

Rachel glanced back. The bee was bigger than any bee she'd ever seen.

"In here, quick!" Mrs Tate called from the side of the field. She pulled open a wooden gate.

They all ran through, then stopped to get their breath.

"I wonder who lives here?" Kirsty said, looking around. They were in a beautiful garden. A path led up to a thatched cottage with yellow roses around the door. Just then, a very strange creature came out from behind some trees. It looked like an alien from outer space!

"Oh!" Rachel and Kirsty gasped.

The creature lifted its gloved hands and removed its white helmet to reveal...an old lady! "Sorry if I startled you," she said, smiling. "I do look a bit strange in my beekeeper's suit."

Rachel sighed in relief. It wasn't a space alien after all!

"I'm Mrs Merry," the old lady went on.

"Hello," Rachel said. "I'm Rachel. This is my friend, Kirsty."

"And this is my mum and dad," Kirsty added.

Mr and Mrs Tate greeted Mrs Merry.

Mr Tate ducked as the huge bee zoomed past his ear. "Watch out!" he said.

"Oh, it's that hiveless queen again," said Mrs Merry. She flapped her hand at the bee. "Go on, shoo!"

Rachel watched it swoop over a hedge and disappear.

"Why did the bee chase us?" Kirsty asked.

"I don't think she was chasing you," said Mrs Merry. "She was just heading this way because she's looking for a hive of her own. But all of my hives already have queens. Since you're here, would you like to try some of my honey?" she asked.

"Yes please!" said Rachel.

They followed Mrs Merry across the lawn to a table covered with rows of jars.

Each jar was filled with rich golden honey. Dappled sunlight danced over the jars, making the honey glow.

"Here you are," said Mrs Merry, spooning some honey onto a pretty plate. "Thank you," Rachel said. She dipped her finger into the little pool of honey and popped it into her mouth. The honey was the most delicious she had ever tasted.

Then she felt it begin to tingle on her tongue. "It tastes all fizzy!" she whispered to Kirsty.

Kirsty dipped her finger into the honey too. "Look!" she said.

Rachel saw that the honey was sparkling with a thousand tiny gold lights. She grabbed Kirsty's arm. "Do you think this means—"

"Yes," said Kirsty. Her eyes were shining. "Another Rainbow Fairy must be nearby!"

❀ ✿ ❁

"We have to find out where this honey came from!" Rachel said.

"Yes," Kirsty agreed. "Mum? Can we stay here a bit longer, please?"

"As long as it's OK with Mrs Merry," Kirsty's mum replied.

Mrs Merry beamed. "Of course they can stay," she said.

Mr and Mrs Tate decided to carry on with their walk. "Make sure you come back by lunchtime," Kirsty's mum said.

"We will," Kirsty promised.

"Come along then, girls." Mrs Merry set off across the lawn.

Rachel and Kirsty followed her down the garden. Six wooden hives stood underneath some apple trees.

"Which one did the honey we tasted come from?" Kirsty asked.

Mrs Merry looked pleased. "Did you enjoy it? The honey from that hive tastes especially good at the moment."

"I think we might know why," Rachel whispered to Kirsty.

"Yes," Kirsty agreed. "It could be fairy honey!"

"That's the one," Mrs Merry said, pointing to the bottom of the garden. One hive stood there all alone, beneath the biggest apple tree.

As they drew nearer to the hive, a sleepy buzzing sound drifted up into the air.

"The bees in this hive are very peaceful," said Mrs Merry. "I've never known them to be so happy."

"Can we get a bit closer?" Rachel asked.

"I think it's safe, with the bees so quiet," Mrs Merry decided. "But you had better wear a hood, just in case." She went into a shed and brought out two beekeepers' hoods. "Here you are," she said. Rachel and Kirsty pulled the hoods over their heads. It was a bit stuffy inside but they could see out of the fine netting. They moved closer to the hive.

The soft buzzing sounded almost like music.

"We need to open it and have a look," Kirsty whispered to Rachel.

Rachel nodded.

But they couldn't start searching for the Yellow Fairy with Mrs Merry there.

Kirsty had an idea. "Could I have a drink of water, please?" she asked.

"Of course you can, dear," Mrs Merry said. She went off towards the cottage.

"Quick!" Kirsty spun round. "Let's open the hive."

Rachel grasped one side of the lid. Kirsty took hold of the other side. It slowly came loose with strings of golden honey stretching down.

"Watch out. It's very sticky," Rachel said.

The girls laid the heavy lid carefully on the ground. Kirsty wiped her fingers on the grass.

"Look!" Rachel whispered.

Kirsty turned to see, and gasped.

A shower of sparkling gold dust shot up out of the hive, shimmering and dancing in the sunlight. Fairy dust!

Rachel peered down into the hive. A tiny girl was sitting cross-legged on a piece of honeycomb, in the middle of a sea of honey.

A bee lay with its head in her lap while she combed its silky hair. Several other bees were waiting their turn, buzzing gently.

"Oh, Kirsty," Rachel whispered. "We've found another Rainbow Fairy!"

The fairy had bright yellow hair. She wore a necklace of golden raindrops around her neck and sparkly golden bracelets on her wrists. Her bright yellow T-shirt and shorts were the colour of buttercups.

"Thank you for finding me!" the fairy called up to them. "I'm Saffron the Yellow Fairy."

"I'm Rachel," said Rachel.

"And I'm Kirsty," said Kirsty. "We've met two of your sisters already – Ruby and Amber."

Saffron beamed. "You've found Ruby and Amber?" She stood up, gently pushing the bee away.

"Yes. They're safe in the pot-at-the end-of-the-rainbow under the willow tree," Rachel said.

Saffron clapped her tiny hands. "I can't wait to see them again." Suddenly she looked worried. "Have you seen any of Jack Frost's goblins near here?"

"No, not here," Kirsty said. "But there were some by the pot yesterday."

"Goblins are scary," Saffron said in a trembling voice. "I've been safe from them here with my friends the bees."

"It's all right," said Rachel. "King Oberon sent one of his frog footmen to look after you and your sisters."

Saffron looked more cheerful.

A large bee crawled from one of the waxy openings in the honeycomb next to Saffron. "This is my best friend, Queenie," said Saffron. She put her arms round the bee's neck and kissed the top of her furry head. Queenie buzzed softly.

"She says hello," said Saffron.

"Hello, Queenie," said Kirsty and Rachel.

Saffron picked up her tiny comb and began to comb Queenie's shiny hair. Another bee buzzed crossly.

"Don't worry, Petal, I'll comb your hair next," Saffron said.

Rachel and Kirsty looked at each other in dismay. Why wasn't Saffron flying out of the hive?

"What if Saffron wants to stay with Queenie and the other bees?" Kirsty whispered.

"Saffron, you have to come with us!" Rachel burst out.

"Or Fairyland will never get its colours back!" Kirsty added. "It will take all of the Rainbow sisters to undo his spell."

"Yes, of course! We have to break Jack Frost's spell!" Saffron cried. She jumped to her feet and picked up her wand.

Suddenly an icy wind sprung up. Something crunched under Kirsty's feet. The grass was covered with frost!

Rachel shivered as something soft and cold brushed against her cheek. A snowflake in summer? "What's happening?" she cried.

"Jack Frost's goblins must be near," Kirsty said.

Saffron's tiny teeth chattered. "Oh, no! If they find me, they will stop me getting back to Fairyland!" Kirsty looked at Rachel in alarm. "Quick, we must go!" Rachel leaned down and carefully lifted the fairy out of the hive. Saffron's golden hair dripped with honey.

"Oh dear, you're really sticky," Rachel said.

Just then Kirsty spotted Mrs Merry coming out of her cottage. Rachel popped the fairy into the pocket of her shorts.

"Hey! It's dark in here!" Saffron complained.

"Sorry," Rachel whispered. "I'll get you out again in a minute."

Suddenly Kirsty noticed the open hive. "We have to put the top back on!" she said.

Rachel helped her lift it and they put it back just as Mrs Merry came through the trees.

"Here's your drink, dear," said Mrs Merry, holding out a glass to Kirsty. She had taken off her strange suit, and in her other hand she was carrying a shopping basket.

"Thank you very much," Kirsty said.

"Now, you girls stay as long as you like," said Mrs Merry. "I've just remembered I must go and buy some fish for my cat."

Rachel watched the old lady go towards the garden gate. Then she slipped her hand into her pocket. "You can come out now," she said to Saffron.

The fairy was covered with grey fluff from Rachel's pocket. "Achoo!" she sneezed. She brushed crossly at the bits of fluff clinging to her wings. "I won't be able to fly!" she wailed.

"We need to clean you up," Rachel said. "But we'll have to be quick, in case the goblins find us."

Kirsty spotted a bird bath filled with clear water. "We could use that."

"Just what we need," Rachel agreed. She carried Saffron over to the bird bath. Saffron fluttered on to the edge of the bath, put down her wand and dived in. Splash!

The water fizzed and turned bright yellow. Lemony-smelling drops shot everywhere.

Sparkling clean, Saffron zoomed up into the air to dry. "That's better!" she cried.

Her wings flashed like gold in the sun as she swooped onto Rachel's shoulder.

"Goodbye, Queenie!" Saffron called.

Queenie looked out of the entrance to the hive. Her feelers drooped sadly as she waved a tiny leg and buzzed goodbye.

As they headed into the woods, Saffron gave a cry and flew up into the air. "Oh, no!" she gasped. "I've left my wand beside the bird bath!"

Rachel looked at Kirsty in dismay. "We'll have to go back," she said.

"Yes," Kirsty agreed. "We can't leave a fairy wand lying about. It would be terrible if the goblins found it."

"Oh, dear... Oh, dear..." Saffron murmured. She fluttered anxiously above them as they went back along the path. Rachel paused at the gate. There was no sign of any goblins.

They ran through the apple trees, straight to Queenie's hive.

Suddenly an icy blast made them all shiver. They gazed around in alarm. Icicles hung from the apple trees, and the lawn was white with frost. The goblins had arrived! Saffron gave a cry of horror. An ugly, hook-nosed goblin jumped up on top of Queenie's hive. He was holding Saffron's wand!

❀ ✿ ❀

"Give me back my wand!" Saffron demanded.

"Come and get it!" yelled the goblin. He leaped off the hive and ran towards the garden gate.

Kirsty gasped as another goblin jumped down from the apple tree. Splat! He landed on the frosty grass and set off at a run.

"Catch!" The goblin threw the wand to his friend. It flew through the air, shooting out yellow sparks.

The other goblin reached up and caught the wand. "Got it!"

Just then, Queenie flew out of the hive. All the other bees swarmed behind her in a noisy cloud.

With Queenie in the lead, the bees formed into an arrow shape and surged after the goblins.

"Be careful, Queenie!" pleaded Saffron.

The goblin shook Saffron's wand at Queenie. "Go away!"

More yellow sparks shot out of the wand. One of the sparks hit Queenie's wing. Queenie wobbled in mid-air. Then she buzzed and flew at the goblin again.

"Help!" The goblin ducked and dropped the wand.

"Butterfingers!" grumbled the other goblin, scooping it up.

"They're getting away!" Kirsty said in dismay.

"No, they're not!" Rachel cried. The cloud of bees shot across the garden and the goblins disappeared under an angry, black cloud.

"Get off me!" spluttered the goblin with the wand. He tried to brush the bees away, but tripped over his feet. As he fell, he bumped into the other goblin. They tumbled in a heap, dropping the wand on to the grass.

"That was your fault!" complained one of the goblins.

"No, it wasn't!" snapped the other one.

Queenie zoomed over and picked up the wand. She carried it to Saffron, who was standing on Rachel's hand.

Saffron took her wand from Queenie and waved it in the air. A fountain of fluttering yellow butterflies sparkled around them.

"My wand is all right!" Saffron cried joyfully.

"Look! The goblins are going," Kirsty said.

The bees had chased the goblins to the end of the garden. Still arguing, they ran across the fields.

As the grumbling voices faded away, the icy wind dropped. The sun shone warmly and the frost melted. The bees streamed back and flew around Rachel and Kirsty, buzzing softly.

"Thank you, Queenie!" Saffron hugged her friend.

Suddenly Queenie wobbled and tipped sideways. Rachel cupped her hands, worried that Queenie would roll off.

"I think she might be hurt," she said.

Saffron knelt down and looked closely at Queenie. "Oh, no!" she gasped. "She's torn her wing!"

"Can you mend Queenie's wing with magic?" Kirsty asked.

Saffron shook her head. "Not on my own. But Amber or Ruby might be able to help me. We must take Queenie to the pot-at-the-end-of-the-rainbow!"

Rachel and Kirsty hurried into the woods. Saffron flew behind them, her rainbow-coloured wings shimmering.

Kirsty went over and parted the branches of the willow tree. A large, green frog hopped out from behind the black pot.

"Bertram!" Saffron flew down and hugged him. "I'm so glad you're here!"

Bertram bowed. "Hello, Miss Saffron. Miss Ruby and Miss Amber will be delighted to see you."

Suddenly a shower of red and orange fairy dust shot up out of the pot, followed by Ruby and Amber.

"Saffron!" Ruby shouted.

"It's good to have you back," Amber called happily, doing a backflip.

The air around the fairies fizzed with red flowers, orange bubbles and yellow butterflies.

Ruby flew on to Kirsty's shoulder. "Thank you, Rachel and Kirsty," she said. She spotted Queenie sitting on Rachel's hand. "Who is this?"

"This is Queenie," Saffron explained. "She helped me get my wand back. But one of the goblins hurt her wing. Can you help?"

Amber frowned. "I could mend Queenie's wing if I had a fairy needle and thread," she said. "But I don't have any here on the island."

Rachel remembered something. "Kirsy! What about the magic bags that the Fairy Queen gave us?"

Kirsty took out her bag. When she opened it a cloud of glitter shot up into the air.

"There's something inside," Kirsty said. She drew out a tiny, shining needle, threaded with fine spider silk. She held it out to Amber.

"Perfect!" Amber said.

She carefully wove the needle in and out of the tear. The row of stitches glowed like tiny silver dots.

Queenie buzzed softly and flapped her wings. Then she zoomed into the air. Her wing was as good as new!

"You have been such a good friend to Saffron, you must stay with us," said Amber, flying up and hugging the bee.

"Yes!" Ruby agreed. "Please come and live with us in the pot."

Queenie flew down and buzzed in Saffron's ear.

"She says she would love to," said Saffron. "There is a hiveless queen in Mrs Merry's garden who will take care of her bees." Then her face fell. "But what about our sisters? They are still trapped!"

"Don't worry," Kirsty said. "We'll find them soon."

"Yes, we will," Rachel agreed. "Nothing will stop us finding all the Rainbow Fairies!"

Fern

the Green

Fairy

Chapter Four

Fern the Green Fairy

"Oh!" Rachel gasped. "What a perfect place for a picnic!"

"It's like a secret garden," Kirsty said, her eyes shining.

They were standing in a large garden. Roses grew around the trees, and marble statues stood half hidden by trailing ivy. Right in the middle of the garden was a crumbling stone tower.

"There was a castle here once called Moonspinner Castle," Mr Walker said. "All that's left is the tower."

"It's just like Rapunzel's tower," Kirsty said. "I wonder if we can get up to the top?"

"Let's go and see!" Rachel said. "Can we, Mum?"

"Off you go," smiled Mrs Walker. "We'll have our picnic when you come back." Rachel and Kirsty rushed over to the door in the side of the tower.

Kirsty tugged at the heavy iron handle. But the door was locked.

"That's a shame," Rachel said.

Kirsty sighed. "Yes, I was hoping Fern the Green Fairy might be here. We have to find her today!"

"Fern," Rachel called in a low voice. "Are you here?"

Here... Here... Here...

Her words echoed off the stones.

Kirsty gasped. "Rachel, look at the ivy!"

Glossy green leaves grew thickly up the tower, but in one place the stones were bare, in the shape of a perfect circle.

"It's just like a fairy ring!" Rachel said. She ran round the tower to take a closer look, and almost tripped over the lace of one of her trainers.

"Careful!" Kirsty said, grabbing Rachel's arm.

Rachel sat down on a mossy stone to retie her shoelace. "There's green everywhere," she said. "Fern must be here."

"We'd better find her quickly then," Kirsty said. "In case Jack Frost's goblins find her first!"

"Where shall we start looking?" Rachel asked, standing up again.

Kirsty laughed. "You've got green stuff all over you!" she said.

Rachel twisted round to look. The back of her skirt was green and dusty. "It must be the moss," she grumbled, brushing it off.

The dust flew up into the air, sparkling in the sun. As it fell to the ground, tiny green leaves appeared and the smell of freshly cut grass filled the air.

Rachel and Kirsty turned to each other. "It's fairy dust!" they gasped.

They walked all round the tower, looking under bushes and inside flowers. But the Green Fairy was nowhere to be found.

Rachel felt very worried. "You don't think the goblins have caught her, do you?"

"I hope not," replied Kirsty. "I'm sure Fern was here, but now she's somewhere else."

She looked down at the tiny leaves. Some of them had begun to flutter across the garden. "I know, let's follow the fairy dust."

The leaves floated over to a path that led into a beautiful orchard.

"It's a magic trail!" Rachel breathed.

They set off along the path, which twisted and turned through the trees.

Suddenly the path opened out into a large clearing. Thick, green hedges loomed above them, their leaves rustling softly.

"It's a maze!" Kirsty cried.

"Look!" Rachel said. "The fairy trail goes right into the maze!"

"We'll have to follow it," Kirsty said bravely.

They followed the floating fairy leaves through the entrance. Kirsty felt a bit scared as the fairy dust led them first one way, then another. What if the trail ran out and they got lost in the maze?

They turned another corner and found themselves in the very centre of the maze, next to a pretty nut tree. The fairy dust led right to the bottom of the tree.

"Fern must be here!" Rachel said.

"Yes, but where?" Kirsty said, looking round.

Tap! Tap! Tap!

"What was that?" Rachel gasped.

Tap! Tap! Tap!

Kirsty pointed at the nut tree. "It's coming from over there."

"I hope it isn't a goblin trap," Rachel whispered.

Tap! Tap! Tap!

Rachel and Kirsty walked right round the tree. At first they couldn't see anything unusual.

Then Rachel noticed something strange. There was a small knot halfway up the trunk – and it was covered by a glass window!

Kirsty touched the window. It was cold and wet. "It's not glass," she whispered. "It's ice!"

Suddenly, something moved behind the icy window. Kirsty could just make out a tiny girl dressed in glittering green.

"Rachel, we've found her!" she said. "It's Fern the Green Fairy!"

Fern waved to the girls through the sheet of ice. Her mouth opened and closed, but Rachel and Kirsty couldn't hear what she was saying. The ice was too thick.

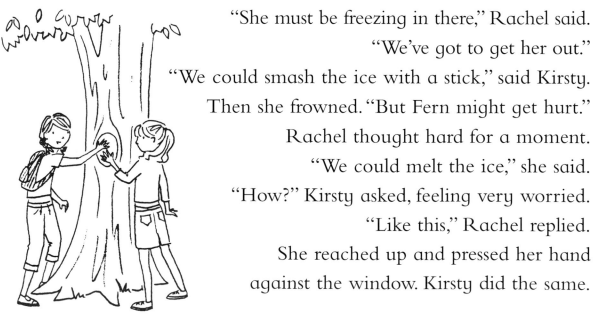

"She must be freezing in there," Rachel said. "We've got to get her out."

"We could smash the ice with a stick," said Kirsty. Then she frowned. "But Fern might get hurt."

Rachel thought hard for a moment.

"We could melt the ice," she said.

"How?" Kirsty asked, feeling very worried.

"Like this," Rachel replied.

She reached up and pressed her hand against the window. Kirsty did the same.

The ice felt freezing cold, but they kept on pressing with their warm hands.

Soon, a few drops of water began to trickle down the window.

"It's melting!" Rachel said. She gently poked the window with her finger and the ice began to crack.

"Don't worry, Fern," cried Kirsty. "You'll be out of there very soon!"

With a crack, the ice split open. A flash of sparkling fairy dust shot out.

And then Fern the Green Fairy pushed her way out of the window, her wings fluttering limply. She wore a bright green top and stretchy trousers, decorated with pretty leaf shapes. She had green pixie boots, and earrings and a pendant that looked like little green leaves. Her brown hair was tied in bunches, and her emerald wand was tipped with gold.

"Oh, I'm s-s-so c-c-cold!" the fairy gasped. She floated down to rest on Kirsty's shoulder.

"Let me warm you up," said Rachel. She scooped the fairy up in her hands and blew gently on her.

Fern stopped shivering, and her wings straightened out. "Thank you," she said. "I feel much better now."

"I'm Rachel and this is Kirsty," Rachel said. "We're here to take you to the pot-at-the-end-of-the-rainbow."

"Ruby, Amber and Saffron are waiting for you," Kirsty added. Fern's green eyes lit up. "They're safe!" she exclaimed. "That's wonderful!" She flew off Rachel's hand and twirled joyfully in the air. "But what about my other sisters?"

"Don't worry, we're going to find them too," Kirsty told her. "How did you get stuck behind the ice window?"

"When I landed on Rainspell Island, I got tangled up in the ivy on the tower," Fern explained. "I untangled myself, but then Jack Frost's goblins chased me. So I ran into the maze and hid in the nut tree. But it was raining, and when the goblins went past, the rainwater turned to ice. So I was trapped."

Rachel shivered. The sun had disappeared behind a cloud, and there was a sudden chill in the air. "It's getting colder," she said.

"The goblins must be close by!" Kirsty gasped.

Fern nodded. "Yes, we'd better go to the pot at once," she said. "You know the way, don't you?"

Rachel and Kirsty looked at each other.

"I'm not sure," Kirsty said. "Do you know, Rachel?"

Rachel shook her head. "We'll have to follow the fairy trail back to the start of the maze."

Kirsty looked around. "Where is the fairy trail?"

An icy breeze was blowing, and the green fairy leaves were drifting away.

"Oh no!" Kirsty gasped. "What are we going to do now?"

Suddenly they heard the sound of heavy footsteps coming through the maze.

"I know that fairy is in here somewhere," grumbled a loud, gruff voice.

"Goblins!" whispered Rachel in dismay.

Rachel, Kirsty and Fern listened in horror as the goblins came closer. As usual, they were arguing with each other.

"Come on!" snorted one goblin. "We can't let her get away again."

"Stop bossing me about," whined the other one.

"Let's hide in the tree," Fern whispered to Rachel and Kirsty. "I'll make you fairy-sized, so we can all fit under a leaf."

Quickly she sprinkled the girls with fairy dust. Rachel and Kirsty gasped as they felt themselves shrinking, down and down.

Fern took the girls' hands. "Let's go," she said, and the three of them fluttered up to a branch. Fern heaved up the edge of a leaf, which was as big as a tablecloth, and they all crept underneath.

A moment later, the goblins rushed into the clearing.

"Where can that fairy be?" grumbled one of them. "I know she came this way!"

"How are we going to get back to the pot?" Rachel whispered to Fern.

Fern pointed past them. "Don't worry! I think I know someone who can help us!"

Rachel and Kirsty turned to look. A furry, grey face was peeping round the tree trunk. It was a squirrel.

"Hello," Fern called softly.

The squirrel jumped and hid behind the trunk. Then he peeped out again, his dark eyes curious.

"Maybe he'd like a hazelnut?" Kirsty suggested.

There was a big, shiny nut growing right next to her. She wrapped her arms around it, but she couldn't pull it off the twig. Rachel and Fern came to help. All three of them tugged at the nut until it came off the branch.

Fern held it out to the squirrel. "Mmm, a yummy nut!" she said.

The squirrel ran lightly along the branch. He took the hazelnut and held it in his front paws.

"What's your name?" asked Fern.

"I'm Fluffy," squeaked the squirrel, between nibbles.

"I'm Fern," said the fairy. "And these are my friends, Rachel and Kirsty. Will you help us get away from the goblins?"

"I don't like goblins," Fluffy squeaked.

"We won't let them hurt you," Fern promised. "Can you give us a ride on your back out of the maze? You can jump from hedge to hedge much better than we can!"

"Yes, I'll help you," Fluffy agreed, finishing the last piece of nut.

Rachel, Kirsty and Fern climbed on to the squirrel's back. It was like sinking into a big, soft blanket!

"This is lovely," said Fern, snuggling down. "Let's go, Fluffy!"

Rachel, Kirsty and Fern clung tightly to Fluffy's fur as he jumped out of the tree, right over the goblins' heads! He landed neatly on the nearest hedge. The goblins were so busy arguing, they didn't even notice.

Fern leaned forward to whisper in the squirrel's ear. "Well done, Fluffy. Now the next one!"

Rachel gulped when she saw how far away the next hedge was. "Maybe Fluffy needs some fairy magic to help him," she said.

"No, he doesn't," Fern replied, her green eyes twinkling. "He'll be fine!"

Fluffy leaped into the air and landed safely on top of the next hedge. Rachel and Kirsty grinned at each other. This was so exciting! The squirrel went so fast, it wasn't long before they had left the goblins far behind.

"Now which way do we go?" Fern said as Fluffy reached the edge of the maze.

"This isn't the way we came in," Rachel said. "I don't know the way to the pot from here. Do you, Kirsty?"

Kirsty didn't know either. But she had an idea. "What about looking in our magic bags?"

Fluffy scrambled down to the ground, and Rachel, Kirsty and Fern climbed off his back. Kirsty opened her rucksack and looked inside. One of the magic bags was glowing with a silvery light.

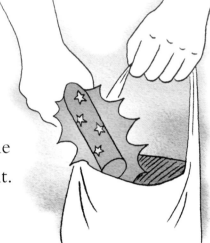

She pulled out a thin, green tube, covered with sparkling gold stars.

"It looks like a firework," Rachel said. "That's not much use, is it?"

"It's a fairy firework!" said Fern. "We can shoot it into the sky, and my sisters will see it from the pot. Then they'll know we need help."

"But won't the goblins see it too, and know where we are?" said Rachel.

"We've got to take the risk," Fern said.

Kirsty stuck the firework into the ground, then she and Rachel moved away. Fern hovered over the firework. She touched the top with her wand and quickly flew back to the girls.

With a loud fizz the firework shot upwards, trailing bright green sparks behind it. It climbed higher and higher, until it burst in a shower of emerald stars. The stars spelt out the words

HELP
WE'RE LOST

Rachel and Kirsty wondered what was going to happen. How could the fairies come to their rescue? They weren't supposed to leave the clearing where the pot was, in case the goblins found them. Suddenly, there was a rustle of leaves behind them.

"Did you see that fairy firework?" shouted a loud voice. "It came from over there!"

Rachel and Kirsty stared at each other in alarm. The goblins were on their trail!

"Don't worry," Fern said. "My sisters will send help quickly."

Rachel spotted a line of golden sparkles twinkling through the fruit trees. "What's that?" she whispered.

"Is it goblin magic?" Kirsty asked anxiously.

Fern shook her head. "They're fireflies!

My sisters must have sent them to show us the way back to the pot."

Suddenly there was another shout from inside the maze. "Look at those lights!"

"The goblins have spotted the fireflies!" Rachel gasped.

"Quick, Fluffy!" Fern said, as they climbed on to the squirrel's back again. "Follow the fireflies!"

The golden specks danced away through the trees. Fluffy scampered after them, just as the goblins dashed out of the maze. "There's the fairy!" one of them shouted. "Stop that squirrel!"

Rachel, Kirsty and Fern clung to Fluffy's fur as the squirrel scrambled up the trunk of the nearest tree. He was just about to jump across to the next tree, when someone called to them from below.

"Hello!"

"Who's that?" Rachel asked. She, Kirsty and Fern peered down at the ground.

A hedgehog was standing at the foot of the tree. "The animals in the garden would like to help get back to the pot," he called.

"Oh, thank you," Fern replied. Then she gasped as the goblins appeared among the trees.

"Where's that squirrel gone?" one of them yelled.

Fluffy leaped across to the next apple tree. The goblins roared with rage and dashed forward. At that very moment, the hedgehog curled himself into a ball and rolled into their path. He looked like a prickly football.

"OW!" both goblins howled. "My toes!"

Rachel and Kirsty laughed as the goblins jumped around holding their feet. "Hooray for Hedgehog!" the girls shouted.

As Fluffy jumped from one fruit tree to the next, the firefly lights behind them began to go out.

"Hey! Who turned off the lights?" wailed one of the goblins. "Which way are we supposed to go?"

"How do I know?" snapped the other goblin. Their voices were getting fainter now as Fluffy hurried on.

"Thank you, fireflies," called Fern, waving at the last few specks of light. "Now we need to find a way to the orchard wall."

"I can help you," a small voice whispered. A fawn was standing at the bottom of the tree. She stared up at them with big, brown eyes. "I can show you a short cut."

She trotted off through the trees. Fluffy leaped from branch to branch above the little deer's head. Rachel could hardly believe she was riding on a squirrel's back, being shown the way to the pot-at-the-end-of-the-rainbow by a fawn! A few moments later they reached the wall which ran round the orchard. On the other side of the wall was a meadow, and beyond that a wood.

"Look!" Rachel shouted. "That's where the pot is!"

"Thank you!" Kirsty and Rachel called to the baby deer. She blinked her long eyelashes at them, and trotted away.

A blackbird hopped over to them, his head on one side. "I'm here to take you to the pot-at-the-end-of-the-rainbow," he chirped. "All aboard!"

Fluffy looked sad as Fern, Rachel and Kirsty slid off his back and climbed onto the blackbird. His feathers felt smooth and silky after Fluffy's fur.

"Goodbye, Fluffy!" called Rachel. She felt sad to leave their new friend behind.

"Look for the big weeping willow tree," Rachel told the blackbird as he swooped across the meadow.

The blackbird landed in the clearing near the willow tree.

"Who's there?" croaked a stern voice. A plump, green frog hopped out from under the tree.

"Bertram, it's me!" Fern called. She waved her wand, and Rachel and Kirsty shot up to their normal size.

"Miss Fern!" Bertram said joyfully. "You're back!"

"Thank you for sending the fireflies," Fern said, giving the frog a hug.

"We saw the firework in the sky," Bertram explained, "so we knew you were in trouble. You'll be safe here," he added.

Rachel and Kirsty pulled aside the long branches to find the pot.

Suddenly a fountain of red, orange and yellow fairy dust whooshed out. Ruby, Amber and Saffron flew into the air with a queen bee behind them.

"Fern!" Ruby called. "It's so good to see you!"

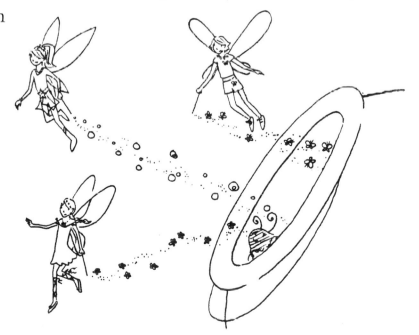

81

Rachel and Kirsty beamed as the fairies hugged each other. The air fizzed and popped with red flowers, green leaves, tiny, yellow butterflies and orange bubbles.

"We've really missed you," said Saffron. Beside her, the bee nudged her with a tiny feeler. "Oh, sorry, Queenie," said Saffron. "This is my sister, Fern."

"How did you get back so quickly?" asked Amber.

"Our woodland friends helped us," Fern said. "Especially Fluffy the squirrel." She sighed. "It was a shame we had to leave him behind."

"Who's that then?" Ruby asked, pointing at a tree.

Fluffy was peeping out from behind the trunk.

"Fluffy!" Fern flew over and hugged him. "What are you doing here?"

"I wanted to make sure you got back to the pot safely," Fluffy explained shyly.

"Would you like to stay with us?" asked Amber.

"Yes, please," squeaked Fluffy.

Fern fluttered onto Rachel's shoulder. "We'll see you again soon, won't we?"

"Yes, of course," Rachel promised.

"And there's only three Rainbow Fairies left to find!" Kirsty added with a grin, before she took Rachel's hand and they ran out of the clearing.

Sky the Blue Fairy

Chapter Five

Sky the Blue Fairy

"The water's really warm!" laughed Rachel. She was sitting on a rock, swishing her toes in a rock pool. Her friend Kirsty was looking for shells nearby.

"Mind you don't slip!" called Mrs Tate. She was sitting on the beach with Rachel's mum.

"OK, Mum!" Kirsty yelled back. As she looked down at her bare feet, a patch of green seaweed began to move. There was something blue and shiny underneath the seaweed.

"Rachel!" she shouted. Rachel went over to Kirsty. "What is it?" she asked. Kirsty pointed to the seaweed. "There's something blue under there," she said. "I wonder if it's..."

"Sky the Blue Fairy?" Rachel said eagerly.

The seaweed twitched.

"Maybe the fairy is all tangled up," Rachel whispered. "Like Fern when she landed on the ivy in the tower."

Fern was the Green Rainbow Fairy. Rachel and Kirsty had already found Fern and her sisters Ruby, Amber and Saffron.

Suddenly a crab scuttled out from under the seaweed. It was bright blue and very shiny. It didn't look like any of the other crabs on the beach.

Kirsty and Rachel smiled at each other. This must be more of Rainspell Island's special magic!

"Fairy in trouble!" the crab muttered. His voice sounded like two pebbles rubbing together.

"Did you hear that?" Rachel gasped.

The crab stopped and peered up at the girls with his little stalk eyes. Then he stood up on his back legs.

"What's he doing?" Kirsty said.

The crab pointed his claw towards some rocks. He scuttled away a few steps, then came back and looked up at Rachel and Kirsty again.

"I think he wants us to follow him," Rachel said.

"Yes! Yes!" said the little crab, clicking his claws. He set off sideways across a large flat rock.

Kirsty turned to Rachel. "Perhaps he knows where Sky is!"

"I hope so," Rachel replied.
The crab scuttled across
a stretch of sand.

"Rachel, Kirsty, it's
nearly lunchtime!" called
Mrs Walker. "We're going
back to Dolphin Cottage."

Kirsty looked at Rachel
in dismay. "But we have
to stay here and look for
the Blue Fairy. What shall we do?"

The crab jumped up and down, kicking up tiny puffs of sand.

"Follow me, follow me!" he said impatiently.

"Could we have a picnic here instead,
please?" Rachel called back.

Mrs Walker smiled. "Of course!
I'll pop back to the cottage with
Kirsty's mum and fetch some sandwiches."

"We'd better hurry," Kirsty said to Rachel. "They'll be back soon."

The crab set off again over a big slippery rock. Rachel and Kirsty
climbed carefully after him. Rachel saw him stop
by a small pool with lots of pretty pink shells.

"Is the fairy in this rock pool?"
she asked.

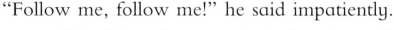

The crab looked into the pool. He scratched
the top of his head with one claw, looking puzzled.
Then he scuttled away.

"I guess not," Kirsty said.

"What about here?" Rachel said, stopping by another pool. This one had tiny silver fish swimming in it.

The crab shook his claw at them and kept going.

"Not this one either," said Kirsty.

Suddenly Rachel spotted a large pool all by itself. "Let's try that one," she said.

They ran over and looked into the water. The sky was reflected in the pool like a shiny, blue mirror.

The crab scuttled up behind them. When he dipped his claw into the pool, the water fizzed like lemonade.

The crab lifted his claw out of the water. Blue sparkles dripped off it and landed in the pool with a sizzle. The entire pool was shimmering with magic!

"Thank you, little crab," Rachel said. She crouched down and stroked the top of the crab's smooth, shiny shell. The crab waved one claw at her, then dived into the water.

He sank to the bottom and scuttled under some seaweed.

Kirsty peered into the pool. "Can you see the Blue Fairy?"

Rachel shook her head.

Kirsty felt disappointed. "I can't either."

"Do you think Jack Frost's goblins have found her?" Rachel said.

Kirsty shuddered. "I hope not!"

Just then, they heard a sweet voice singing. "With silver bells and cockle shells, and pretty maids all in a row..."

"Do you think it's the little crab?" Rachel whispered.

Kirsty shook her head. "His voice was all gritty."

"Yes," said Rachel. "This sounds more like a fairy!"

"I think the singing is coming from that seaweed," said Kirsty.

Rachel peered into the pool. "Look!" she said.

A huge bubble came bobbing out of the seaweed and floated towards the surface.

Rachel and Kirsty stared in astonishment. There was a tiny girl inside the bubble!

"I think we've found Sky the Blue Fairy!" Kirsty gasped.

The fairy pressed her hands against the sides of the bubble. She wore a short, sparkly dress and knee-high boots the colour of bluebells. Her earrings and hairband were made of tiny stars, and she

was holding a silver wand. "Please help me!" Sky said in a tiny voice like bubbles popping. Suddenly, a cold breeze stirred Rachel's hair. A dark shadow fell across the pool and the glowing blue water turned grey.

Rachel looked up. The sun was still shining brightly. "What's happening?" she cried.

There was a strange hissing, crackling sound. A layer of frost crept across the rocks towards them, covering the beach in a crisp, white blanket.

"Jack Frost's goblins must be very near," Kirsty said.

Ice began to cover the pool.

"Oh, no!" cried Rachel. "Sky's going to be trapped!"

Sky's bubble stopped bobbing. It hung very still, frozen into the ice. Sky looked very scared.

"We have to rescue her!" Kirsty exclaimed.

"How can we melt the ice?" Rachel wondered anxiously.

"Why don't we look in our magic bags?" said Kirsty. Rachel frowned. "Oh, no! I've left them in my rucksack on the other side of the rock pools! I'll run back and fetch them."

Kirsty blew on her hands to warm them. "I'll stay here. But hurry!"

89

"I won't be long," Rachel promised. She scrambled back over the rocks and onto the sandy beach. Her rucksack was lying where she'd left it. She took out one of the magic bags. It was glowing with a soft golden light. When she opened it, a cloud of glitter sprayed out.

Rachel slipped her hand into the bag. There was something inside that felt smooth and shiny. It was a tiny blue stone, shaped like a raindrop.

Rachel felt very puzzled. It was pretty, but how could it help?

The blue stone began to glow in her hand, hotter and hotter until it was almost too warm to hold. As it grew hotter, it glowed fiery red. Rachel grinned. They could use it to melt the ice and set Sky free!

She ran back as fast as she could. But

when she reached the frozen pool, Kirsty wasn't on her own any more. Two ugly hook-nosed goblins were skating on the ice! "Shoo! Go away!" Kirsty shouted at them. "Go away yourself!" one of the goblins yelled rudely, sliding away from her.

90

Kirsty tried to grab the other goblin. But he dodged away. "Can't catch me!" he shouted.

"Hee, hee! The fairy's stuck in the ice!" laughed the other goblin, doing a little twirl.

"We're going to get her out!" Kirsty told him. "We're going to find all the Rainbow Fairies!"

"Oh no, you won't," said the goblin. He stuck out his tongue.

"Jack Frost's magic is too strong," said the other goblin. "Hey, look at me!" He held out his arms and slid across the ice on one foot. But the ice was very slippery. He crashed right into his friend.

Splat!

"Clumsy!" the goblin snapped.

"You should have moved out of the way," grumbled the other one, rubbing his bottom.

The goblins tried to stand up. But their feet skidded sideways and they fell over again.

91

Rachel saw her chance. She threw the magic blue stone onto the ice.

A shower of golden sparks shot into the air and the stone glowed bright red. A big hole appeared in the centre of the pool.

"Ow! Hot! Hot!" yelled the goblins. They scrambled to the edge of the pool and rushed away, their big feet slapping on the rocks.

"They've gone!" Kirsty said in relief.

Rachel peered into the pool. "I hope Sky isn't hurt," she said.

All the ice had melted and the water reflected the blue sky once again. Sky's bubble was floating just below the surface.

Rachel saw Sky sit up inside the bubble and look around. She looked very pale.

Kirsty put her hand in the water. It was still warm from the magic stone. Very gently, she poked her finger into the bubble to burst it.

Pop!

Sky tumbled free of the bubble and swam up to the surface, her golden hair streaming behind her.

Kirsty leaned over and fished the fairy out. She felt like a tiny wet leaf. Kirsty put her on a rock in the sun. "There you are, little fairy," she whispered.

Sky propped herself up on one elbow. "Thank you for helping me," she said weakly. Water dripped from her hair and her wings, but there were no blue sparkles.

Kirsty frowned. "All the fairies we found before had fairy dust. What has happened to Sky's sparkles?"

"I don't know," said Rachel. "And she's so pale, almost white."

It was true. You could hardly tell Sky's dress was blue at all.

Kirsty bit her lip. "It looks as if Jack Frost's magic has taken away her colour!"

The little crab scuttled out of the water and made his way across the rock to Sky. "Oh dear, oh dear," he muttered. "Poor little fairy."

Sky shivered. "I'm so cold and sleepy," she sighed.

"What's the matter, Sky?" said Kirsty. "Did the goblins get too close to you?"

Sky nodded. "Yes, and now I can't get warm." She curled up in a tiny ball and closed her eyes.

Rachel felt very scared. Poor Sky looked really ill!

"Don't worry," the crab said in his gritty voice. "My friends will help us."
He scuttled up to the top of the rock and snapped his claws.
"What's he going to do?" Kirsty wondered. Then she stared in amazement.

Lots and lots of crabs were coming out of the rock pools around them. Big ones, little ones, all different colours.

The blue crab pointed up at the sky, then down at the ground. His friends pattered away in all directions. Their little stalk eyes waved as they prodded their claws into the cracks between the rocks.

"What's going on?" said Rachel.

Kirsty spotted a tiny pink crab tugging and tugging at something. With a gritty crunch, the crab tumbled over backwards. It held a fluffy white seagull feather in its claws. The crab scrambled up again, waving the feather in the air.

One by one, the other crabs searched out more feathers and brought them over to the rock where Sky lay. Very carefully, the blue crab tucked the feathers round Sky.

"They're trying to warm Sky up with seagull feathers!" Kirsty said. There were so many feathers now that Rachel couldn't see the fairy at all.

Would the blue crab's idea work? she wondered.

There was the tiniest wriggle in the feather nest. A faint puff of blue sparkles fizzed up, smelling of blueberries. One pale blue star wobbled upwards and disappeared with a pop.

"Fairy dust!" Rachel whispered.

"But there's not very much of it," Kirsty pointed out.

There was another wriggle from inside the nest. The feathers fell apart to reveal the Blue Fairy, her dress still very pale. She opened her big, blue eyes and sat up.

"Hello, I'm Sky the Blue Fairy. Who are you?" she said.

"I'm Kirsty," said Kirsty.

"And I'm Rachel," said Rachel.

"Thank you for frightening the goblins away," said Sky. "And thank you, little crab, for finding all these lovely, warm feathers." She tried to unfold her wings, but they were too crumpled. "My poor wings," said the fairy, her eyes filling with tiny tears.

"The feathers have helped, but Sky still can't fly," Kirsty said.

"Maybe the other Rainbow Fairies can help," Rachel said.

"Do you know where my sisters are?" Sky asked.

"Oh, yes," said Kirsty. "So far, we've found Ruby, Amber, Saffron, and Fern."

"They are safe in the pot-at-the-end-of-the-rainbow under the willow tree," Rachel added.

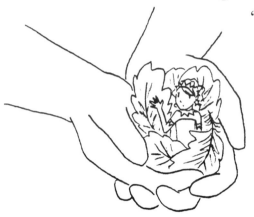

"Could you take me to them, please?" said Sky. "I'm sure they will make me better." She tried to stand up, but her legs were too wobbly and she had to sit down again.

"Here, let me carry you," Rachel offered. She cupped her hands and scooped up the feather nest with the fairy inside.

Sky waved at the little blue crab and his friends. "Goodbye. Thank you again for helping me."

"Goodbye, goodbye!" The blue crab waved his claw. His friends waved too, their little stalk eyes shining proudly.

Kirsty and Rachel glanced at each other as they crunched across the pebbles. The goblins had got closer to Sky than any of the other Rainbow Fairies. And now the Blue Fairy was hardly blue at all!

☆ ☆ ☆

Rachel and Kirsty hurried into the woods. Rachel carried Sky very carefully. The fairy lay curled in a ball, her cheek resting on her pale hands.

"Here's the glade with the willow tree," Kirsty said when they reached the clearing. The scent of oranges hung in the air, tickling their noses. Rachel looked round and spotted a fairy hovering over a patch of daisies, collecting nectar in an acorn cup.

"Look!" Rachel said. "It's Amber the Orange Fairy."

Amber fluttered over and settled on Rachel's shoulder. "Hello again!"

Then she saw Sky lying curled in the feathers. "Oh, no! What's happened? I must call the others," she cried. She waved

her wand and a fountain of sparkling orange dust shot into the air.

The other Rainbow Fairies fluttered up all over the clearing. The air sparkled with red, orange, yellow, and green fairy dust. Bubbles and flowers, tiny butterflies and leaves sprinkled the grass.

97

The fairies clustered around Sky. The Blue Fairy sat up and gave a weak smile, then flopped back into her nest of feathers.

"Why is she so pale?" Saffron asked.

"The goblins got really close to her," Rachel explained. "They froze the pond. Sky was trapped in a bubble under the ice."

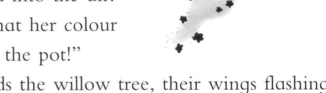

Saffron shuddered. "That's terrible!"

Ruby the Red Fairy zoomed into the air. "We must warm Sky up so that her colour comes back. Let's take her to the pot!"

The fairy sisters sped towards the willow tree, their wings flashing. Rachel and Kirsty carried Sky over in her feathery nest.

As Rachel put Sky down beside the pot, a large green frog hopped out.

"Miss Sky!" he croaked.

Sky gave another weak smile. "Hello, Bertram."

"We have to make Sky warm so she gets her colour back,"

Fern explained. Bertram looked very worried. "Jack Frost's goblins are so cruel," he said. "You must stay close to the pot, Fairies, so that I can protect you."

"Don't worry, Sky," said Saffron, giving her a hug. "You'll soon feel better."

Sky didn't answer. Her eyes started to close. She was so pale, her arms and legs seemed almost transparent.

"Oh Bertram, what can we do to help Sky?" Fern gasped.

Bertram looked very serious. "I think it's time for you all to try a spell."

Amber frowned. "It might not work with only four of us. Rainbow Magic needs seven fairies!"

"Bertram's right, we have to try," Ruby said. "Quick, let's make a fairy ring."

The Rainbow Fairies fluttered into a circle above Sky.

Rachel noticed a black-and-yellow queen bee and a small grey squirrel appear at the edge of the glade. "Queenie and Fluffy have come to watch," she whispered to Kirsty.

Ruby lifted her wand.

"*In a fairy ring we fly,*

To bring blue colour back to Sky!" she chanted.

The fairies waved their wands. Four different colours of dust sparkled in the air – red, orange, yellow, and green. The dust covered Sky in a glittering cloud.

"Something's happening!" Kirsty said. She could see that Sky's short dress and knee-high boots were turning bluer and bluer. "The spell is working!"

Whoosh!

A shimmering cloud of blue stars shot into the air.

"We did it!" cheered Amber, turning a cartwheel in the air.

"Hooray for Rainbow Magic!" cried Ruby.

Sky yawned and sat up. She brushed the feathers away and looked down at herself. Her face lit up. Her dress was blue again!

"My wings feel strong enough to fly now," she said.

She flapped them twice, then zoomed into the air.

The Rainbow Fairies clustered round Sky. The air bubbled with fairy dust – red, orange, yellow, green and blue. It was nearly a whole rainbow!

Rachel and Kirsty beamed.

"You won't need these any more!" Fern laughed, tickling Sky with a long, white seagull feather.

"But I think I might know what to do with them!" said Sky. She gathered up the rest of the feathers. "We could put these on our bed. They'll be very warm and soft."

"That's a very good idea," said Ruby.

"Let's have a welcome home feast," said Fern. "With wild strawberries and clover juice."

Amber did another cartwheel. "Yippee! Rachel and Kirsty, you're invited too!"

"Thank you, but we have to go." Rachel looked at her watch. "Our mums will be waiting with our picnic."

"Oh, yes!" Kirsty remembered. She would love to taste some fairy food but she didn't want her mum to be worried. "Goodbye, we'll be back again soon!"

The fairies sat on the edge of the pot and waved to the girls. "Goodbye! Goodbye!"

Sky fluttered beside Rachel and Kirsty as they walked across the glade. Her dress and boots glowed bright blue, and blueberry scent filled the air.

"Thank you so much, Rachel and Kirsty," she said. "Now five Rainbow Fairies are safe." As they made their way back to the beach, Rachel looked at Kirsty. "Do you think we can find Izzy and Heather in time? The goblins nearly caught Sky today!" Kirsty smiled. "Don't worry. Nothing is going to stop us from keeping our promise to the Rainbow Fairies!"

Izzy
the Indigo
Fairy

Chapter Six

Izzy the Indigo Fairy

"Rain, rain, go away," Rachel Walker sighed.

She stared out of the window of her attic bedroom. Raindrops splashed against the glass, and the sky was full of purply-black clouds.

"And what about Izzy the Indigo Fairy?" Kirsty said. "We have to find her today."

"Remember what the Fairy Queen said?" Rachel reminded Kirsty.

Kirsty nodded. "She said the magic would come to us."

"That's right," Rachel said. "What shall we do while we're waiting?"

Kirsty went over to the bookshelf and pulled one out. It was so big, she had to use two hands to hold it.

The Big Book of Fairy Tales, Rachel read, looking at the cover.

Kirsty grinned. "If we can't find fairies, at least we can read about them!"

She was about to turn the first page when Rachel gasped. "Kirsty, look at the cover! It's purple. A really deep bluey-purple."

"That's indigo," Kirsty whispered. "Do you think Izzy could be trapped inside?"

"Let's see!" Rachel said.

Kirsty opened the book. She thought that Izzy might fly out of the pages, but there was no sign of her. On the first page was a picture of a wooden soldier. Above the picture were the words: *The Nutcracker.*

"I know this story," Rachel said. "A girl called Clara gets a wooden nutcracker soldier for Christmas. He comes to life and takes her to the Land of Sweets."

On the next page there was a picture of snowflakes swirling through a forest.

"Aren't the pictures great?" Kirsty said. "The snow looks so real." Rachel put out her hand and touched the page. It felt cold and wet. "It is real!" she gasped.

Kirsty looked down at the book again. The snowflakes started to swirl up from the pages, into the bedroom. Soon the snowstorm was so thick, Rachel and Kirsty couldn't see a thing.

They were swept up into the air by the spinning snow cloud.

Rachel yelled to Kirsty, "Why haven't we hit the bedroom ceiling?"

"Because it's magic!" Kirsty cried.

Suddenly the snowflakes stopped swirling. Rachel and Kirsty were standing in a forest, with their rucksacks at their feet. Trees loomed around them and snow covered the ground.

"This is the forest in the picture," Rachel said. "We're inside the book!" Then she frowned. There was something odd about this snow. She bent down and touched a snowdrift. "This isn't snow," she laughed. "It's icing sugar!"

Kirsty scooped up a handful and tasted it. The icing sugar was cool and sweet.

Rachel could see a pink and gold glow through the trees. "Let's go and see what that is," she said.

They picked up their rucksacks and set off. *Crack!*

Rachel nearly jumped out of her skin as a loud noise echoed through the trees.

"Sorry," said Kirsty. "I trod on a twig."

"Wait," Rachel whispered. "I just heard voices!"

"Goblins?" Kirsty whispered back, looking scared.

Rachel listened. "No, they sound too sweet and soft to be goblins."

They hurried towards the edge of the forest. When they came out of the trees, they saw that the glow was coming from a dazzling pink and gold archway.

"Look!" Rachel gasped. "It's made of sweets!"

The archway was made of pink marshmallows and golden toffees.

Then they heard the voices again. Two people wearing fluffy white coats were chatting to each other as they scooped icing sugar into shiny metal buckets. They had rosy cheeks and pointy ears. They were so busy they hadn't noticed Rachel and Kirsty yet.

"I think they're elves," Kirsty whispered. "But they're the same size as we are. That means we must be fairy-sized – or, at least, elf-sized – again."

"But we haven't got any wings this time," Rachel pointed out.

Suddenly one of the elves spotted them. "Hello!" she called.

"Who are you?"

"I'm Rachel and this is Kirsty," Rachel explained.

"Where are we?" Kirsty asked.

"This is the Land of Sweets," said the first elf. "My name is Wafer, and this is my sister, Cornet."

"We're the ice-cream makers," added Cornet. "What are you doing here?"

"We're looking for Izzy the Indigo Fairy," Kirsty told them. "Have you seen her?"

The elves shook their heads. "We've heard of the Rainbow Fairies," said Wafer. "But Fairyland is far away from here, across the Lemonade Ocean."

"Maybe you should ask the Sugarplum Fairy for help," Cornet suggested. "She lives on the other side of the village."

The elves led Rachel and Kirsty through the archway of sweets.

On the other side of the arch, the sun shone warmly. Flowers made of strawberry cream grew beneath milk-chocolate trees. Pink and white marshmallow houses lined the street, which was paved with boiled sweets.

"Isn't this great?" Kirsty laughed. "It's like being inside a giant sweet shop!"

"And it all looks yummy!" Rachel agreed. There were elves hurrying everywhere. Some had shiny buckets like the ice-cream

makers, and others carried tiny hammers. There were gingerbread men too, looking very smart with their bright bow ties and currant buttons. A tiny pink sugar mouse scampered across the street,

looking very sweet.

Suddenly a cross-looking gingerbread man hurried out of one of the houses.

"Hello, Buttons," Wafer said. "What's the matter?"

"Look at my best bow tie!" said the gingerbread man, holding it out. "It was red when I hung it out to dry, and now it's changed colour!"

Rachel and Kirsty gasped. The bow tie was bluey-purple!

"Izzy!" they said together.

The ice-cream elves looked puzzled. "I think this means that Izzy the Indigo Fairy is close by," Rachel explained. "We'd better help you find her before she gets into trouble," Cornet said.

A small elf ran towards them. He had one hand clapped over his mouth.

"That's our little brother, Scoop," Wafer explained to Rachel and Kirsty. "Scoop, what are you up to?"

Laughing, Scoop took his hand away from his mouth. His lips were indigo!

"I had a drink from the lemonade fountain," he giggled. "All the lemonade's turned bluey-purple. It made my tongue tingle, too!"

"That sounds like more Rainbow Fairy magic!" Kirsty said.

"Where's the lemonade fountain?" Rachel asked.

"In the village square," replied Cornet. "Just round the corner."

"Thanks for your help," said Kirsty. She grabbed Rachel's hand and they ran off.

As soon as Rachel and Kirsty rounded the corner, they skidded to a halt. Bluey-purple liquid bubbled up from a dolphin-shaped fountain

in the middle of the square. A crowd of elves and gingerbread men stood round the fountain, all talking at once. They sounded cross.

110

A swirl of indigo fairy dust shot up from the middle of the crowd. As the dust fell to the ground, it changed into dewberry-scented inkdrops.

Rachel and Kirsty grinned. They had found another Rainbow Fairy!

"Izzy!" Rachel called, as she and Kirsty pushed their way through the crowd. "Is that you?"

"Who's that?" called a cheerful voice.

Izzy was standing next to the lemonade fountain. She had neat blue-black hair and twinkling, dark blue eyes. She was dressed in indigo denim jeans and a matching jacket, covered with spangly patches. Inkdrop-shaped silver earrings hung in her ears, and her wand was indigo, tipped with silver.

"Who are you?" Izzy said. "And how do you know my name?"

"I'm Kirsty, and this is Rachel," Kirsty said. "We've come to take you back to Rainspell Island."

"We've found five of your sisters," Rachel added.

"That's brilliant news!" Izzy cried.

111

"How did you get to the Land of Sweets?" Kirsty asked.

"The wind blew me down the chimney of Mermaid Cottage, and into the story of *The Nutcracker*," Izzy said.

Before Rachel and Kirsty could say anything else, the crowd started shouting.

"Look what she's done to the lemonade fountain!" grumbled one elf.

"I didn't mean to," Izzy said. "The lemonade looked so yummy, I had to have a drink. That's when it turned indigo."

"What about my bow tie?" snapped Buttons.

"I was tired," Izzy said. "I borrowed your lovely bow tie to wrap round me while I had a nap."

The crowd started to mutter again.

"Wait," Rachel said. "Have you heard about Jack Frost's wicked spell?"

The crowd listened while Rachel told them the whole story. When she'd finished, they didn't look cross any more.

"I'm sorry for all the trouble I've caused," Izzy said. "Please can you tell us how to get back to Rainspell Island?"

"The Sugarplum Fairy will help you," said a Jack-in-the-Box. "She lives just past the jellybean fields."

"Come on, then!" Izzy cried. She took Rachel and Kirsty by the hand.

"Good luck!" called everyone. Rachel, Kirsty and Izzy walked along the road towards the jellybean fields. Just outside the village was a rock of golden toffee, as tall as a marshmallow house. Elves were tapping the rock with little hammers to break off pieces of toffee.

Other elves picked them up and put them into silver buckets.

"That looks like hard work," Kirsty said. "They don't seem to be collecting much toffee at all!"

Rachel peeped into one of the buckets as an elf walked past. Kirsty was right. There were only a few chips of toffee in it.

"Is there something wrong with the toffee?" Izzy wondered.

The elf with the bucket overheard her. "It's really hard today," he grumbled. "Anyone would think it had been frozen."

"Frozen!" Kirsty said in alarm. "Do you think that means Jack Frost's goblins are here?"

"I hope not," Izzy said.

Just then, there was a loud, rumbling noise and a shout of "Look out!" An enormous wooden barrel was rolling straight towards them!

And two goblins were running behind, grinning all over their ugly faces.

Izzy gave Rachel and Kirsty a push. "Quick! Get out of the way!"

They jumped aside just in time.

Crash!

The barrel smashed right into the toffee mountain and burst open. Lemon sherbet spilled out in a sticky yellow cloud.

"Izzy! Kirsty!" Rachel coughed. "Are you all right?"

"I think so!" Kirsty sneezed. "Atishoo!"

"HELP!"

Kirsty heard Izzy's frightened voice. But she couldn't see her through the sherbet cloud.

"Help!" Izzy shouted again. "The goblins have got me!" Her voice was getting fainter.

"Quick, Rachel!" Kirsty gasped. "Have you got our magic bags?"

Still coughing, Rachel swung her rucksack off her back. Inside, one of the magic bags was glowing. Rachel pulled out a folded paper fan. Puzzled, she opened the fan up.

It was coloured like a rainbow, with stripes of red, orange, yellow, green, blue, indigo and violet. Rachel began to flap the fan at the clouds of sherbet.

Whoosh!

A blast of air from the fan blew all of the sherbet away.

"This fan is amazing!" Rachel gasped.

"Look!" shouted Kirsty.

The goblins had tied Izzy's trainers together with strawberry bootlaces. They were half-dragging, half-carrying her up the road.

"We've got to save her," Rachel said, folding the fan and putting it in her pocket.

"I'll go and tell the Sugarplum Fairy," said one of the elves.

Rachel and Kirsty ran up the road. The goblins had a head start, but Izzy was wriggling so much that she slowed them down.

The road led through the jellybean fields. Tall green plants stood in rows, each one covered with different-coloured beans. Elves were picking the jellybeans and putting them into baskets.

One of the goblins skidded to a halt. He grabbed a handful of beans from the nearest plant.

The other goblin did the same. "Yummy!" said the first goblin, stuffing the beans into his mouth. "They're so greedy, they're stealing the jelly beans!" Rachel panted. "Yes, but it gives us a chance of catching them up!" Kirsty puffed.

The elves in the field shouted angrily at the goblins. But that didn't stop them. They were picking beans with one hand and holding on to Izzy with the other.

"I've got an idea," Rachel whispered. She lifted up a basket full of beans which had already been picked.

"Look what I've got," she called. "A whole basket full of beans!"

The goblins' eyes lit up.

"Those jellybeans look yummy," Izzy said to the goblins. "I wish I could have one."

"Be quiet," snapped a goblin. He turned to the other goblin. "You hold the fairy while I get the basket."

"No," said the other one. "You'll eat all the beans! You hold the fairy, and I'll get the basket."

"No!" roared the first goblin. "Then you'll eat all the beans!"

Glaring at each other, both goblins let go of Izzy and ran towards Rachel.

She threw a handful of beans on the ground and backed away.

The goblins bent down to grab the beans. When they stood up again, Rachel threw another handful down the hill, away from Izzy. While the goblins were busy stuffing themselves, Kirsty rushed over to untie Izzy.

"Are you all right?" she asked.

Izzy wriggled her feet. "Yes, thank you!"

Rachel left the basket on the ground and ran over to Kirsty and Izzy. The goblins began squabbling over the rest of the beans.

"Let's get out of here!" Rachel said.

Suddenly there was a gentle flapping noise. Rachel looked up to see a butterfly with pink and gold wings fluttering above them. On its back sat a fairy with long, red hair.

The butterfly landed on the ground. The fairy climbed off the butterfly's back and smiled at Izzy and the girls. She wore a long green and gold dress and a tiara. "Welcome," she said. "I am the Sugarplum Fairy." She looked sternly at the goblins. "What are you doing in the Land of Sweets?" she demanded.

The goblins didn't answer. They were too busy groaning and holding their tummies.

"My tummy hurts," moaned one goblin.

"Mine too," whined the other one. "I feel sick."

Izzy grinned at Rachel and Kirsty. "They've eaten too many jellybeans!"

The Sugarplum Fairy looked even crosser. "As you have stolen so many of our delicious jellybeans," she said to the goblins, "you must be taught a lesson."

"Why don't you make them pick jellybeans?" Izzy suggested.

"What a good idea," smiled the Sugarplum Fairy.

The goblins looked horrified at the thought of more jellybeans! Several elves came running out of the jellybean fields. They marched the goblins into the nearest field and handed them empty baskets.

With sulky faces, the goblins started to pick the beans. "Serves them right for being greedy!" laughed Izzy.

"Please can you help us get back to Rainspell Island?" Rachel asked the Sugarplum Fairy. The beautiful fairy nodded.

"We will send you home by balloon!" she said. She waved her wand at the empty bean basket.

Rachel and Kirsty watched in amazement as it grew bigger and bigger.

"There is your basket," said the Sugarplum Fairy.

"But where's the balloon?" said Rachel.

The Sugarplum Fairy pointed to a tree covered with pink blossoms.

"What pretty flowers," Kirsty said. She took a closer look and laughed. "They're not flowers. They're pieces of bubblegum!"

Rachel felt puzzled. "How is that going to help?"

Izzy grinned, her eyes sparkling. "Leave it to me!" she said.

She pulled one of the bubblegum flowers off the tree, popped it into her mouth and began to chew.

Screwing up her face, she blew a huge, pink bubblegum bubble.

She puffed and puffed, and the bubble grew bigger and bigger. Soon it was the biggest bubblegum bubble Rachel and Kirsty had ever seen! Izzy took the bubble out of her mouth and tied a knot in the end. "The perfect balloon!" she said. "Now we're ready to go."

Rachel and Kirsty beamed at each other. What a brilliant way to travel back to Rainspell!

The elves working in the jellybean fields, and the elves who had followed Rachel and Kirsty out of the village, helped to tie the bubblegum balloon to the basket. Then Rachel, Kirsty and Izzy climbed inside.

The Sugarplum Fairy waved her wand at the balloon, showering it with gold sparkles.

"The balloon will take you to Rainspell Island," she said.

"Thank you," called Rachel and Izzy.

Kirsty looked round in dismay. "But there's no wind to make us fly!"

Rachel looked at the leaves on the bubblegum tree. Kirsty was right. They weren't moving at all.

The Sugarplum Fairy smiled. "Rachel, don't you remember what you have in your pocket?" she said. "Of course! The magic fan!" Rachel exclaimed. She took it out of her pocket and flapped it. *Whoosh!*

The blast of air lifted the balloon up into the sky.

"Goodbye!" Kirsty called.

"Thank you for all your help," cried Izzy.

As they bobbed higher, Rachel put away the fan. Big, puffy clouds swirled around the balloon and the wind roared, rocking the basket from side to side. Rachel, Kirsty and Izzy hung on to each other.

All of a sudden, the wind dropped.

Kirsty opened her eyes.

"We're home!" she gasped.

They were back in Rachel's attic bedroom at Mermaid Cottage. The balloon and the basket had vanished. The book of fairy tales was lying on the floor.

"Where's Izzy?" Rachel said.

"I'm in here!" said a cheeky voice. The Indigo Fairy popped up from Rachel's pocket. She fluttered into the air, showering the room with fairy dust inkdrops. Kirsty picked up the book and found a picture of the Land of Sweets.

"It's a shame we didn't get to taste any of the sweets," she said.

A puff of icing sugar floated out of the book and a shower of jellybeans fell on to Rachel's bed.

"They must be a present from the Sugarplum Fairy!" laughed Izzy.

Rachel and Kirsty each popped a jellybean into their mouths. They were tiny, but they tasted lovely!

"Yum!" said Izzy, munching a bean. "Can we take some for my sisters?"

Rachel nodded. "Let's go right away," she said, filling her pockets with beans. She looked at Kirsty and smiled. They had rescued another fairy and escaped the goblins once again. They'd even been inside a fairy story in a book. And now there was only one more fairy to find!

Heather
the Violet Fairy

Chapter Seven

Heather the Violet Fairy

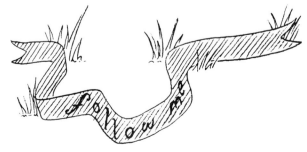

"I can't believe this is the last day of our holiday!" said Rachel. She watched her purple kite soar in the clear blue sky above the field beside Mermaid Cottage.

"But we still have to find Heather the Violet Fairy!" Kirsty reminded her. Rachel felt the kite tug on its string. Something violet and silver flashed at the end of its long tail. "Look!" she gasped.

"What is it?" Kirsty said.

"Do you think it's a fairy?"

"I'm not sure," Rachel said, winding in the string.

As the kite bobbed towards them, Kirsty saw that a long piece of violet-coloured ribbon was tied to its tail.

"It has tiny silver writing on it," Rachel said.

Kirsty crouched down to look closer. "It says, 'Follow me'."

Suddenly the ribbon was lifted up by the breeze. It fluttered across the field.

"It must be leading us to Heather!" Kirsty said.

"Mum, is it OK if we go exploring one last time?" Rachel called.

Mrs Walker was talking to Kirsty's mum outside Mermaid Cottage.

"Of course, if Kirsty's mum agrees," Mrs Walker replied.

"Yes, but don't go far," said Mrs Tate. "The ferry leaves at four o'clock."

"We'll have to hurry!" Rachel whispered to Kirsty.

They ran through the grass, following the ribbon.

Suddenly it vanished behind a hedge.

Rachel and Kirsty squeezed through the branches. Luckily the leaves weren't too prickly. On the other side they found a path, and a gate. There was a sign on the gate, in purple paint, saying: SUMMER FAIR TODAY!

The girls went through into a pretty garden. Candyfloss and ice-cream stalls stood at the edge of a smooth green lawn. There were people everywhere, chatting and laughing. Kirsty spotted the ribbon fluttering towards a merry-go-round at the far end of the lawn. It wrapped itself round the golden flagpole and danced in the breeze like a tiny flag.

"It must be leading us to the merry-go-round!" Kirsty said.

The merry-go-round was as pretty as a fairy castle. Rachel stared with delight at the wooden horses on their shiny golden poles.

"Hello there!" called a friendly voice. "I'm Tom Goodfellow. Do you like my merry-go-round?"

Rachel and Kirsty turned to see an old man with white hair and a kind smile.

"It's lovely," Rachel said.

"Look, Rachel," Kirsty gasped. "The horses are all rainbow colours! Red, orange, yellow, green, blue, indigo and violet."

The merry-go-round slowed down and the music stopped.

Rachel noticed that the pillar in the centre was decorated with a picture of rainbow-coloured horses galloping along a beach.

"All aboard for the next ride!" Mr Goodfellow called. He smiled down at Rachel and Kirsty. "How about you two?" he asked, his blue eyes twinkling.

❀ ❀ ❀

"We'd love to have a go!" said Kirsty. "Quick, Rachel, there are two horses left!" She scrambled on to one of them. A name was painted in gold on its bridle.

"My horse is called Indigo Princess," Kirsty said, stroking the horse's shiny coat.

Rachel climbed on to a pretty horse next to Kirsty's. It had a lilac-coloured coat and a silver mane. "Mine is called Prancing Violet."

"Hold tight everyone!" Mr Goodfellow called out.

The music started and the merry-go-round began to turn.

Prancing Violet and Indigo Princess swooped up and down on their poles.

Rachel laughed as they spun faster and faster. The garden flashed by, and the flowers and paths disappeared in a blur. The sounds of music and laughter faded away.

Rachel's heart skipped. The only horse she could see was Kirsty's horse, Indigo Princess. And she could feel Prancing Violet's hooves thudding on the ground beneath her!

Kirsty felt a breeze tugging at her hair. Indigo Princess seemed to toss her head and kick up sand as she galloped along. "This is like riding a real horse!" she exclaimed.

The horses began to slow down. The beach faded away, and the sound of music returned. The merry-go-round came to a smooth halt.

Kirsty patted Indigo Princess's neck as she dismounted. "Thanks for the special ride!" she whispered. Then she turned to Rachel. "This merry-go-round is definitely magical, but where is Heather the Violet Fairy?"

"I don't know," Rachel said. Then she heard the tiniest tinkling laugh behind her.

Rachel turned round. There was nobody there, just the picture on the pillar in the middle of the merry-go-round.

Rachel blinked. There was a fairy riding the violet-coloured horse! She wore a short, floaty, purple dress, long purple stockings, and ballet slippers. Purple flowers were tucked behind her ear.

"Kirsty!" Rachel whispered. "I think I've just found Heather the Violet Fairy!"

"Heather must be trapped in the painting on the pillar!" Kirsty said. "We've got to get her out!"

"But how?" Rachel said. "What can we do with all these people here?"

Just then, Mr Goodfellow clapped his hands. "Follow me, everyone. The clowns are here!"

Everyone cheered and scrambled off the merry-go-round. Rachel and Kirsty were left alone.

"Now's our chance!" Kirsty said.

"Let's use our magic bags," Rachel said.

Kirsty put her hand in her pocket and took out her magic bag. When she opened it, a cloud of glitter fizzed into the air. There was something long and slim inside. It was a tiny golden paintbrush.

Kirsty frowned. "We don't want to paint any more pictures."

"Maybe Heather knows what we can use it for," Rachel said.

"Good idea," Kirsty said. As she bent closer to the picture on the pillar, the brush touched the painted fairy's hand. Suddenly, the whole picture glowed, and the fairy's tiny fingers moved!

"Look!" Rachel gasped. "She's coming alive!"

"The brush is working magic on the painting!" Kirsty whispered.

She began to stroke the brush round the outline of the fairy. The picture glowed even brighter.

"That tickles!" said the fairy with a silvery laugh.

With Kirsty's last stroke, the fairy sprang out of the painting. Purple fairy dust shot everywhere, turning into violet-scented blossom.

"Thank you for rescuing me!" said Heather. "I'm Heather the Violet Fairy! Do you know where my Rainbow sisters are?"

"I'm Rachel, and this is Kirsty," said Rachel. "Your sisters are safe in the pot-at-the-end-of-the-rainbow, under a willow tree."

Heather did a twirl of delight. "Hooray!"

She landed gently on Kirsty's hand. Kirsty held her out of view until they had run through the garden, past the people watching the clowns.

They ran out of the gate, and down the path that led to the wood. As soon as they reached the clearing, there was a shout from inside the pot. Izzy the Indigo Fairy zoomed out. "Heather, you're safe! Look, everybody! Rachel and Kirsty have found Heather!" Saffron flew out of the pot on the back of a bumble-bee, followed by the other Rainbow Fairies. The air flashed and fizzed with scented bubbles, flowers and leaves, stars, inkdrops and tiny butterflies. Bertram the frog footman hopped out from behind the pot, beaming from ear to ear.

"We knew you were coming," said Amber the Orange Fairy, doing a cartwheel. "I've been tingly with magic all morning!"

131

Rachel and Kirsty held hands and danced in a circle. They had found all seven Rainbow Fairies! Ruby the Red Fairy's wings sparkled as she fluttered down to land on Rachel's shoulder. "Thank you, Rachel and Kirsty," she said.

"You are true fairy friends," agreed Fern the Green Fairy.

Suddenly Rachel heard a strange crackling sound. She spun round. The pond at the edge of the glade wasn't blue any more. It was white and cloudy with ice!

"Goblins!" cried the fairies.

Izzy's tiny teeth chattered. "B-b-but it can't be. The Sugarplum Fairy kept them in the Land of Sweets!"

Just then, a harsh cackling laugh rang out. The bushes parted, and a tall bony fairy walked into the glade. Icicles hung from his clothes and there was frost on his hair and eyebrows.

It was Jack Frost!

❀ ❀ ❀

"So you are all together again!" Jack Frost's voice sounded like icicles snapping.

"Yes, thanks to Rachel and Kirsty," Ruby declared bravely.

"And now we want to go home to Fairyland!" She flew into the air. "Come on, Rainbow Fairies!"

Izzy shot to her sister's side, and turned to face Jack Frost. She looked very determined. The other fairy sisters flew to join them, and they all lifted their wands, chanting together:

"To protect the Rainbow Fairies all,
Make a magic raindrop wall!"

A rainbow-coloured spray shot out of each wand and a shining wall of raindrops appeared between the fairies and Jack Frost.

"It will take more than a few raindrops to stop me!" Jack Frost hissed. He pointed a bony finger at the shimmering wall.

The raindrops turned to ice. They dropped onto the frosty grass like tiny glass beads and shattered.

133

The fairies looked horrified. Saffron and Sky gave a sob of dismay and Izzy clenched her fists. Fern, Amber and Ruby hugged each other.

Heather looked as if she was thinking hard. Then she waved her wand, and cried:

"To stop Jack Frost
from causing trouble,
Catch him in a magic bubble!"

A gleaming bubble popped out of the end of Heather's wand. It grew bigger and bigger.

Jack Frost laughed, and stretched out his icy fingers. But before he could do anything, there was a loud fizzing sound. Jack Frost vanished.

Rachel blinked in surprise.

Heather's spell had trapped Jack Frost *inside* the bubble! The wicked fairy pressed his hands against the pale lilac wall, looking furious.

"Well done, Heather!" Fern exclaimed. "That was very brave!"

"Quick, everyone. We must get into the pot-at-the-end-of-the-rainbow and magic a rainbow to take us back to Fairyland!" Heather urged

Rachel and Kirsty held the branches out of the way so that the fairies could fly through.

A squirrel skittered down the trunk.

"Who are you?" Heather asked.

"This is Fluffy," said Fern, stroking the squirrel.

"Fluffy and Queenie will have to go back to their homes now," said Sky.

"We'll come and visit them, won't we?" Fern said. All the fairies nodded.

Fern reached up to give Fluffy one last hug before he scampered off.

Queenie buzzed goodbye as she flew away.

Heather fluttered in front of Rachel and Kirsty. "Would you like to come to Fairyland with us?" Rachel and Kirsty nodded. Heather waved her wand, sprinkling the girls with purple fairy dust. Kirsty felt herself shrinking. The grass seemed to rush towards her. "Hooray! I'm a fairy again!" she cried. Rachel laughed in delight as wings sprang from her shoulders.

Just then, there was a yell from the giant bubble. Rachel and Kirsty looked round. Jack Frost was looking very scared. His face was bright red and drops of water ran down his cheeks. He was *melting!* Sky's wings drooped. "Without Jack Frost, there will be no seasons. We need his cold and ice to make winter," she said.

"No winter?" Izzy looked shocked. "But I love sledging in the snow and skating on the frozen river."

"Without winter, how can spring follow?" Amber said. "What will happen to all the lovely spring flowers?"

"And the bees need the flowers to make honey in summer," Saffron said sadly. "And in autumn, the squirrels find nuts to store for winter," said Fern. "We have to have all the seasons. But that won't happen if we leave Jack Frost trapped in the bubble."

Heather spoke up. "You're right. But most importantly, I feel sorry for Jack Frost. He looks very frightened."

"We have to do something," said Ruby.

"But he might cast another spell!" Kirsty said.

136

"Even so, we have to help him, don't we?" Amber said. All the other Rainbow Fairies agreed.

Kirsty felt very proud of them. The fairies were being so brave!

Sky hovered over the giant bubble. She whispered her spell so quietly that Rachel and Kirsty couldn't hear the words.

A jet of blue fairy dust streamed out of her wand into the bubble. The dust swirled in a spiral until it filled the whole bubble.

Rachel and Kirsty flew over and peered in.

The fairy dust had turned into huge crystal snowflakes. The water on Jack Frost's face froze. He had stopped melting! The wind whipped the snow faster, spinning Jack Frost in circles.

"Look! He's getting smaller!" Kirsty gasped, pointing to the bubble. Now Jack Frost was smaller than a goblin. Then he was smaller than a squirrel, then even smaller than Queenie the bee! With a loud POP, the bubble burst. The wind dropped and the snow vanished. At first Kirsty thought Jack Frost had completely disappeared. Then she saw a very small glass dome lying on the grass. There was a tiny figure leaping angrily about inside the dome, shaking his fists.

"It's a snow dome!" Kirsty said in amazement. "And Jack Frost's trapped inside!"

❀ ❀ ❀

"Hooray for Sky!" shouted Rachel. "Now we can take Jack Frost safely back to Fairyland." She flew over and picked up the snow dome. It felt smooth and cold, and it trembled when Jack Frost leaped about.

Bertram hopped towards Rachel. "I'll take care of that, Miss Rachel," he said.

"Into the pot, everybody!" shouted Izzy. "It's time to go back to Fairyland!"

"Yippee!" yelled Amber, doing a backflip in mid-air.

Heather waved her wand and the pot rolled on to its four short legs. Rachel, Kirsty and all the fairies flew inside.

Bertram the frog climbed in too. It was a bit of a squash, but Rachel and Kirsty were too excited to mind.

"Ready?" Ruby asked.

Her sisters nodded. The seven Rainbow Fairies raised their wands. There was a flash above them, like a rainbow-coloured firework. A fountain of sparks filled the pot: red, orange, yellow, green, blue, indigo, and violet.

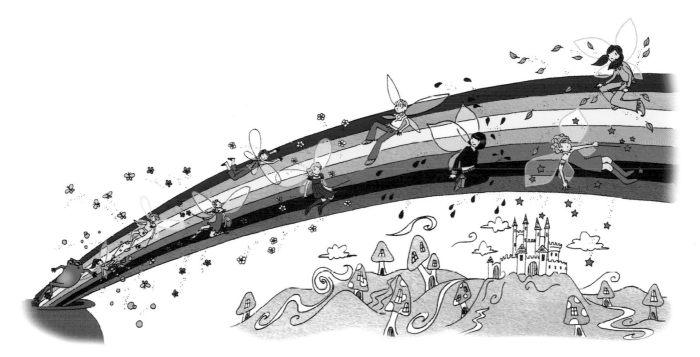

With a whoosh, Bertram and the fairies shot out of the pot, carried on the rainbow like a giant wave. Rachel and Kirsty felt themselves zooming up the rainbow too. Flowers, stars, leaves, tiny butterflies, inkdrops and bubbles fizzed and popped around them.

"This is amazing!" Kirsty shouted.

Far below, she could see hillsides dotted with toadstool houses. It was Fairyland!

All of a sudden, the rainbow vanished in a fizz of fairy dust. Kirsty and Rachel flapped their wings and drifted gently to the ground. Rachel looked around, expecting to see all the colours coming back to Fairyland.

But the hills and the toadstool houses were still grey!

"Why hasn't the colour returned?" Rachel gasped.

One by one, the Rainbow Fairies landed next to them. And Kirsty saw that when each fairy touched the ground, a patch of the greenest green started spreading outwards from their feet.

"Rachel, look!" Kirsty cried. The fairy sisters stood in a circle and raised their wands. A fountain of rainbow-coloured sparks shot up. There was a flash of golden lightning, and it began to rain. Rachel and Kirsty gazed in delight as tiny glittering raindrops, every colour of the rainbow, pattered down around them. Where they fell, the colour returned, flowing like shining paint across everything in Fairyland.

The toadstool houses gleamed red and white. Brightly-coloured flowers dotted the green hillside with orange, yellow and purple.

On the highest hill, the fairy palace shone softly pink. Music came out as the front doors opened.

"Hurry!" Ruby said. "The King and Queen are waiting for us."

Rachel and Kirsty and the seven fairies flew towards the palace.

140

Bertram hurried along below them with enormous leaps. Fairies, elves and pixies rushed out of the palace. "Hooray for the Rainbow Fairies!" they cheered. "Hooray for Rachel and Kirsty!"

Titania and Oberon came out of the palace. "Welcome back, dear Rainbow Fairies," said Titania. Bertram bowed. "This is for you, Your Majesty," he said, giving the snow dome to the King.

"Thank you, Bertram," said Oberon. He looked into the dome. "Now, Jack Frost," he said sternly. "If I let you out, will you promise to stay in your icy castle and not harm the Rainbow Fairies again?"

Jack Frost scowled and didn't answer.

"Remember that winter still belongs to you," Titania said.

"Very well," said Jack Frost. "But on one condition."

"And what is that?" asked Oberon.

"That I'm invited to the next Midsummer Ball," said Jack Frost. Titania smiled. "Of course we'll invite you. You will be very welcome," she said kindly.

Oberon tapped the snow dome and it cracked in half. Jack Frost sprang out and shot up to his full height.

He snapped his fingers and a sledge made of ice appeared next to him. Hopping onto it, he zoomed up into the sky. "Goodbye. We'll see you at the Midsummer Ball!" Sky called after him. Jack Frost looked over his shoulder. A smile flickered across his sharp face, then he was gone.

The Fairy King and Queen smiled at Rachel and Kirsty.

"Thank you, dear friends," said Oberon. "Without you, Jack Frost's spell would never have been broken."

"You will always be welcome in Fairyland," Titania told them. "And wherever you go, watch out for magic. It will always find you." The Rainbow Fairies fluttered over to say goodbye. Rachel and Kirsty hugged them all in turn. They couldn't help feeling sad that their fairy adventures were over.

"Here's a special rainbow to take you home!" said Heather.

The fairies raised their wands one more time. An enormous shining rainbow whooshed upwards.

"Here we go!" Rachel shouted as she felt herself being sucked into the fizzing colours.

"I love riding on rainbows!" said Kirsty.

Soon the holiday cottages appeared below them. They landed with a soft bump behind Mermaid Cottage.

"We're back to our normal size," Rachel said, standing up.

"Just in time to catch the ferry!" Kirsty added as they ran round to the front garden.

"There you are," said Rachel's mum. "Did you see that beautiful rainbow? And it wasn't even raining. Rainspell Island is a really special place!"

Kirsty and Rachel shared a secret smile.

"Check your bedroom to see if you've left anything behind," said Kirsty's mum.

"OK," said Kirsty. She dashed into Dolphin Cottage and went upstairs.

"I'll check mine, too!" Rachel hurried into Mermaid Cottage and ran up to the attic.

She stopped dead in her bedroom doorway. "Oh!" she gasped.

In the middle of the bed, something glittered like a huge diamond.

It was a snow dome, full of fluttering fairy dust shapes.

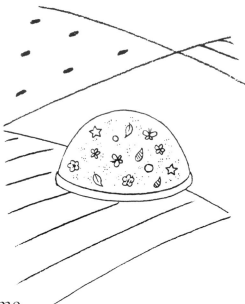

Rachel scooped up the dome and dashed next door.

Kirsty was running downstairs with a matching snow dome.

The two friends beamed at each other. "Every time I shake my snow dome or see a rainbow, it will make me think of the Rainbow Fairies," said Rachel.

"Me too!" replied Kirsty. "We'll never forget our secret fairy friends!"